AMERICAN FOLK SONGS FOR CHILDREN

American Folk Songs
for Children IN HOME, SCHOOL AND NURSERY SCHOOL

A BOOK FOR CHILDREN,
PARENTS AND TEACHERS

by Ruth Crawford Seeger

ILLUSTRATED BY BARBARA COONEY

A ZEPHYR BOOK
Doubleday & Company, Inc., Garden City, New York.

To Michael and Peggy
and Barbara and Penelope

ISBN: 0-385-15788-6
COPYRIGHT © 1948 BY RUTH CRAWFORD SEEGER
LITHOGRAPHED IN THE UNITED STATES OF AMERICA
9 8 7 6 5 4 3

Acknowledgments

I want to thank many more people than can be included on these pages. Traditional singers like Bascom Lamar Lunsford and eighty-year-old Emma Dusenbury. Mothers like Fran Irving and Betty Purcell. An acquaintance who became a friend through the songs, like Rose Alschuler. A personal friend who opened many doors—Vanett Lawler. First, however, my husband, who had talked of gathering together songs like these long before those first weeks at nursery school, back in 1941, when he challenged "Why don't you?" to my hesitation. And the Sandburg family, for my memories of first knowing music like this—memories of spring and fall evenings and a guitar and songs and Lake Michigan below the pine trees. And the Bentons, Tom and Rita, for late hours in their loft down on New York's 8th Street, with harmonicas, guitars, and singing. And with special affection, the Lomax family, for their large part in building and nurturing in me a sense of the variety and aliveness of American folk idioms.

Then, the school in which the book began to grow—the Silver Spring Cooperative Nursery School of Silver Spring, Maryland—for the spirit of adventure with which parents and teachers met the songs and used them. And, at school, Glenore Horne, without whose enthusiasm and instant pleasure in the singing of each new song as it came along, the book might never have been made. And Margaret Fairley, whose thoughts on the delicate balance between tradition and improvisation became so linked with my own that it is hard now sometimes to tell which are hers and which are mine. And Rose Leff Gregg who, knowing how I feel about using the songs, helped and contributed to the writing of several chapters on usage, because she was sure I had not said what I meant to say.

Then my colleague, Laura Pendleton MacCarteney, who gave freely of warm, friendly interest as well as practical professional advice at a time when both were especially needed. And Gertrude Price Wollner, whose pioneer work in music improvisation with children brought us together for long discussions. And Dr. Agnes Greig, for the enrichment of my own insight and for her thoughtful reading of the manuscript. Mary Lemon Lambert, too, for enthusiastic correcting of music proof. And certainly Lilla Belle Pitts, for the picture of herself as a small child running home light-hearted through Mississippi twilight singing "Run, Chillen, Run."

Perhaps most of all, though, the Seeger children Michael and Peggy and Barbara and Penelope, who remember not only singing the songs but numbering pages, punching holes, licking reinforcements, pasting music, typewriting, even proofreading—and finding a sign on the study door when they came home from school: MOTHER WORKING.

And to the following publishers, societies, institutions and individuals, for permission to use the various songs as indicated:

AMERICAN FOLKLORE SOCIETY for "Johnny Get Your Hair Cut" from *Hill Country Tunes* by Samuel Preston Bayard, in the *Memoirs of the American Folklore Society*, Vol. 39; for the following songs from the *Journal of American Folklore*: "Sailing in the Boat" ("Rose in the Garden") from *Song Games from Connecticut* by Emma M. Backus; "Old Mister Rabbit," "Scraping Up Sand in the Bottom of the Sea" ("Shiloh"), and "Yonder She Comes," from *The Missouri Play-Party* by Mrs. L. D. Ames, Vol. 24.

BOTKIN, B. A. for "Buffalo Girls," "Jim along Josie," and "Walk along John" from *The American Play-Party Song*, University of Nebraska Press. Copyright, 1937.

COLLINS, FLETCHER, JR. for "Eency Weency Spider," and "What Shall We Do When We All Go Out?" from *Alamance Play Party Songs and Singing Games*, Elon College, N.C., 1940.

EDDY, MARY O. for "There Was a Man and He Was Mad" from *Ballads and Songs from Ohio*, J. J. Augustin, New York. Copyright, 1939.

FISCHER, CARL for "Turtle Dove" from *30 and 1 Folk Songs from the Southern Mountains*, compiled and arranged by Bascom Lamar Lunsford and Lamar Stringfield. Copyright, 1929.

HARBISON, KATHERINE for "When I Was a Young Maid" from *In the Great Meadow and the Prairie*, in the *Southern Folklore Quarterly*, Vol. II, No. 3.

HARCOURT BRACE AND COMPANY for "By'm Bye" ("Stars Shining"), and "Hanging Out the Linen Clothes" from *The American Songbag* by Carl Sandburg. Copyright, 1927.

HARVARD UNIVERSITY PRESS for "Built My Lady a Fine Brick House," "The Closet Key," "Do, Do, Pity My Case," "Hop Old Squirrel," "Jimmy Rose He Went to Town," "Juba," "Old Aunt Kate," "Old Mister Rabbit," "One Cold and Frosty Morning" ("Old Jessie"), "Lula Gal" ("Tie My Shoe"), "Run, Chillen, Run" ("Run, Nigger, Run"), "Riding in the Buggy, Miss Mary Jane," "This Lady She Wears a

Dark Green Shawl," "Who's That Tapping at the Window," from *On the Trail of Negro Folk Songs* by Dorothy Scarborough. Reprinted by permission of the President and Fellows of Harvard College; for "As I Walked Out One Holiday" ("The Little Boy Threw His Ball So High," or "The Jew's Garden"), "Down by the Greenwood Sidey-o," "Down Came a Lady" ("Lord Daniel's Wife," or "Little Matthew Grove"), "It Rained a Mist" from *Traditional Ballads of Virginia* by Arthur Kyle Davis. Reprinted by permission of the President and Fellows of Harvard College.

INDIANA HISTORICAL COMMISSION for "Such a Getting Upstairs" ("Getting Upstairs") from *The Play-party in Indiana* by Leah Jackson Wolford. Copyright, 1916.

LIBRARY OF CONGRESS, and the collectors and singers of the following songs, transcribed from field recordings in the Archive of American Folklore:

HERBERT HALPERT, collector, for: "Adam Had Seven Sons," "Here Sits a Monkey" ("Here Sits a Lady"), "Oh, John the Rabbit," sung by groups of children in Mississippi.

JOHN A. LOMAX, collector, for: "Baby Dear," sung by Daisy Smith; "Big Old Owl" ("Jim Crack Corn"), sung by Alec Dunford; "Dog Tick," sung by Ray Wood; "How Old Are You" ("Yaddle Daddle"), sung by the Gant family; "I'm Going to Join the Army," sung by J. M. Mullins; "Old Molly Hare," sung by Alec Dunford; "Pretty Little Girl with the Red Dress On" ("Poor Howard"), sung by Leadbelly.

SIDNEY ROBERTSON, collector, for: "Bought Me a Cat," "Did You Go to the Barney," "The Juniper Tree," sung by Emma Dusenbury; "Free Little Bird" and "John Henry," sung by Bascom Lamar Lunsford; "Frog Went a-Courting," "Jesus Borned in Bethlea," sung by S. F. Russell.

CHARLES SEEGER, collector, for: "My Horses Ain't Hungry," "Old Joe Clarke" ("Round and Round"), "Skip-a to My Lou," sung by Rebecca Tarwater.

LOMAX, JOHN A., ESTATE OF, for "All Around the Kitchen" ("Cocky Doodle Doodle Doo"), "Billy Barlow," "Hush Little Baby," "Ducks in the Millpond," "Every Monday Morning" ("John Henry"), "Go to Sleepy," "Going Down to Town" ("Lynchburg Town"), "Have a Little Dog" ("Toll a Winker"), "Little Bird, Little Bird," "The Little Black Train," "Mary Wore Her Red Dress," "Old Blue," "Rain or Shine" ("Doney Gal"), "Sally Go Round the Sunshine" ("Sally Go Round the Moon"), "The Wind Blow East," from *Our Singing Country*, John A. and Alan Lomax, The Macmillan Company. Copyright, 1941; for "Old Molly Hare" and "Pretty Little Girl with the Red Dress On" (see Library of Congress, above).

LUNSFORD, BASCOM LAMAR for "Free Little Bird" and "John Henry," transcribed from recordings made by Sidney Robertson (see Library of Congress, above).

MACCARTENEY, LAURA PENDLETON for permission to adapt "Little Gray Ponies" ("Little Horses") from *Songs for the Nursery School*, The Willis Music Company. Copyright, 1937.

THE MACMILLAN COMPANY for "Goodbye, Julie" ("Miss Julie Ann Johnson") from *Negro Folk Songs as Sung by Leadbelly*, by John A. and Alan Lomax. Copyright, 1936; for "Goodbye, Old Paint," "The Little Pig" ("Tale of a Little Pig"), "Pick a Bale of Cotton," from *American Ballads and Folk Songs* by John A. and Alan Lomax. Copyright, 1934.

MCINTOSH, MR. AND MRS. DAVID S. for "Roll That Brown Jug Down to Town" from *Singing Games and Songs from Southern Illinois*. Cooperative Recreation Service, Delaware, Ohio. Copyright, 1941.

NORTON, W. W. for "Blow, Boys, Blow," and "Fire Down Below" from *Songs of American Sailormen* by Joanna Colcord. Copyright, 1938.

OXFORD UNIVERSITY PRESS, AND MISS MAUD KARPELES for "The Cherry Tree Carol," "What Did You Have for Your Supper" ("Jimmy Randall, My Son"), "Monday Morning Go to School" ("The Two Brothers"), "Rose, Rose and Up She Rises," "Poor Old Crow" ("The Three Ravens"), "What'll We Do with the Baby," from *English Folk Songs from the Southern Appalachians*, collected by Cecil J. Sharp, edited by Maud Karpeles. 1932.

OWENS, WILLIAM A. for "Jingle at the Windows" ("Tideo") from *Swing and Turn: Texas Play-Party Games*, Tardy Publishing Company. Copyright, 1936.

PENN NORMAL, INDUSTRIAL AND AGRICULTURAL SCHOOL, St. Helena Island, N. C. for "I Got a Letter This Morning," "Sweet Water Rolling," "Mary Had a Baby," "When the Train Comes Along," from *Saint Helena Island Spirituals* by N. G. J. Ballanta – (Taylor), G. Schirmer. Copyright, 1925.

SOUTHERN FOLKLORE QUARTERLY for "When I Was a Young Maid" (see Harbison).

TEXAS FOLKLORE SOCIETY for the following songs from the *Publications of the Texas Folklore Society*: "Oh, Oh the Sunshine" ("Oh, Oh You Can't Shine"), "Rain Come Wet Me" from *Old Time Darky Plantation Melodies* by Natalie Taylor Carlisle, Vol. V; two choruses of "Old Joe Clarke" ("Round and Round") from *Some Texas Play-Party Songs* by Dudley and Payne, Vol. I; "Toodala" from *Toodala* by Helen Gates, Vol. XVII.

VIKING PRESS, THE for "Who Built the Ark? Noah, Noah" from *Rolling Along in Song* by J. Rosamond Johnson. Copyright, 1937.

VOSE, ELIZABETH M. for "Hush 'n' Bye" ("All the Pretty Little Horses").

WILKINSON, WINSTON for an excerpt from *Virginia Dance Tunes* in the *Southern Folklore Quarterly*, Vol. 6, No. 1.

Ruth Seeger's songbook is no sudden notion. It represents many years of a rare mother living with her music and her children. Her collection embodies an extraordinary array of time-tested songs for little ones, many of them so old they have been forgotten and now have the freshness of the new.

Carl Sandburg

Preface

Children will take the songs in this book to their hearts, for the young belong to that spiritual fellowship which lives close to the heart of things. On the instant of hearing, children will know that here are songs that will give vitality, beauty, and power to their own emotions, imaginations, and experiences.

Because this is so, *American Folk Songs for Children* is as truly a child's book as it is a book for parents and teachers. For it is made up of songs that have been shaped by folk wisdom. That is, by children and grownups who have been, and continue to be, moved to give voice to what has been felt, heard, seen, and lived through.

Happily, Ruth Crawford Seeger knows in her very bones what folk art *is* and what it *is not*. So the fresh, simple beauty and worth of the material selected have not been spoiled by either an intellectualized attitude or by sophisticated treatment.

As a matter of fact, this is a book, if ever there was one, that has grown out of the very heart of an affectionate and co-operative family and social life. One has to read only the opening chapter—*How the Book Grew*—to feel completely at home, as well as in love, with all who have had a share in its "growing."

What Mrs. Seeger has said in the introductory chapters has all the qualities that make folk songs *good:* freshness, simplicity, human understanding, sincerity, and the rightness of age-old wisdom.

No teacher or parent, interested in making music mean more in the lives of children, can afford to miss the delight that comes from the *rightness* of what is said about the use of these songs in schools and homes. And no teacher who has had misgivings about some of the things done at school in the name of creative expression will fail to gain comfort from the wise counsel to be found in *Improvising on the Words*.

But why go on telling teachers and children and parents why *American Folk Songs for Children* is a treasure? Some of the joy of discovery should be left for the many who have waited a long time for just such a reward.

Whether the takers be young or old—and they are certain to be both—here is a book to warm the hearts of all who are sensitive to the enduring quality of things lovely in themselves.

LILLA BELLE PITTS
Professor of Music Education
Teachers College
Columbia University

Contents

Classified Indices

These songs were sung around home with our own children, and at schools with other children of varying ages. They were gathered together and given simple piano arrangements for use in the Silver Spring Cooperative Nursery School of Silver Spring, Maryland, during its initial year, 1941. They have also been used by Laura Pendleton MacCarteney, and myself, at the National Child Research Center, and by me at the Foxhall Nursery School, the Green Acres School, and, with older children, at the Whitehall Country School, the Georgetown Day School and the Potomac School, all of Washington, D.C. or nearby Maryland.

The songs are folk (traditional) songs—tunes and words—current in various parts of North America where the English language is predominant. They are published here as they were found in the collections and folklore journals from which they were taken or on the phonograph recordings in the Archive of American Folklore in the Library of Congress in Washington. The State in which each song was collected is indicated above its notation. Most of the songs are known in other States as well, either in this or in other versions. Except in a few cases and in small details, changes have not been made either in the music or the words: the stanza which appears as part of the music notation, and any stanzas immediately following the music notation, are traditional or folk texts. Suggestions for improvisation are clearly indicated as such, either by explanatory remarks or headings.

To call the collection a book of songs for children, parents, and teachers is to outline doubly the history of its growth—first, through the experience of two parents with their own children, to whom songs like these were almost as natural as speech; second, through the experience of a parent-teacher with a group of thirty-odd mothers and their children, to many of whom native American music idioms were unfamiliar.

Back as far as our own children can remember, our house has been full of the sound of songs like these—ballads, work songs, love songs, prison songs, dance songs, hollers, chants, spirituals, blues. It was part of my job as music editor of a book of American folk music to transcribe several hundred such tunes from phonographic recordings made throughout the country—along roadsides, in valley and mountain homes, in towns and cities, fields and prisons. Our children would hear one of these songs hours on end—slow, fast, loud, soft, a single phrase repeated over and over until a notation could be devised which would show some of the subtle nuances of the melody and still be easy to read. The song would pursue them through open windows on a summer day while they played. It would travel to them through closed doors in winter while they ate or slept or had the measles. Not infrequently the phonograph would be heard all day and far into the night. Of course I also sang the songs myself. I couldn't help singing them. And that was a good way of trying out the singability of my notations.

So by the time three years had passed and the book had gone to press, Barbara and Peggy and Michael (then three and five and seven) had acted as test tubes for many a song of love, woe, or nonsense (three songs apiece each night if they were in bed on time). The phonograph might have played *Ol' Hannah* half a day—but they wanted it sung to them when bedtime came, and again next morning when Ol' Hannah showed her face above a cold winter horizon. Ol' Hannah is the sun.

> *Go down, Ol' Hannah,*
> *Well . . . well . . . well . . .*
> *Don't you rise no more.*
> *If you rise in the mornin'*
> *Set the world on fire.*

Just as Barbara turned four a co-operative nursery school was in process of getting started in Silver Spring. Barbara and I enrolled. Each mother was expected to participate in the school activities one day a week with her child, and was given special duties. The music program fell to me.

After a few weeks some of our family favorites began to be heard at school—songs like *Skip-a to My Lou, Old Joe Clarke, My Horses Ain't Hungry*. The children liked them. And the mothers liked them. They liked them so much that we decided to try an experimental year during which we would sing chiefly American folk songs. I began to cull, from among the songs I knew and from the many collections of American folk music, from folklore journals and phonographic field recordings at the Library of Congress, songs which would fill our needs. And I found plenty of them—plain tunes, melodically simple, rhythmically vital, whose traditional texts possess the spirit of work and play and thought and speech of small children.

Do we want to sing about rain? Here is an old ballad heard in Virginia for generations (*It Rained a Mist*). Or about wind and sunshine? Here is a Bahaman clapping-and-drumming song (*The Wind Blow East*). Or about trains, or hammers, or color, or sleep, or cooking, or buying things, or going upstairs, or tying shoes? Then here is a spiritual (*The Little Black Train*) and a work song (*This Old Hammer*) and a singing game (*This Lady She Wears a Dark Green Shawl*) and a lullaby (*Go to Sleepy*) and a nonsense song (*Old Aunt Kate She Bake a Cake*) and a dance song (*Going Down to Town*) and a play-party song (*Such a Getting Upstairs*) and another dance song (*Lula Gal*). Do we want to play ball (*Down by the Greenwood Sidey-o*) or turn around and around (*Old Joe Clarke*) or walk or run or skip or jump (*Jim Along Josie*)? Or just sit and count stars (*By'm Bye*)? Here's a song of sailing, and of fire on a ship. Here's a song of a rabbit, a pig, a cat, a free little bird, an old black crow. Here's a song about picking cotton, and selling tobacco, and raising vegetables, and scraping up sand from the bottom of the sea. Here's a family song, with no one left out. And here are songs which can sing about each of us and what he is wearing or seeing or doing or wanting to do—songs which can change with the day and our thoughts.

When the first dozen songs were tentatively selected, a copy was made for each of the two teachers and the six "music mothers" who had volunteered to help with the music on days when I would not be at school. We all met one evening to learn and discuss the new songs, staying till a late hour to swap favorites back and forth to the accompaniment of someone's guitar.

It began to be evident, after that meeting, that the "music mothers" were not the only ones who wanted to sing. Others said: "We like these songs the children are singing; we want to sing them at home. Where are our copies of the music?" So after that we made enough copies for every school mother, with complete text included for adult singing (some stanzas of which might be thought unsuitable for children!). Each new set of a dozen untried songs called for another music meeting: the songs must be learned and their uses discussed from various angles—musical, textual, educational.

To these meetings came a good third of the school mothers, together with teachers and a somewhat reluctant volunteer to stay outdoors with the children while everyone else sang and talked. Thus a fair percentage of the mothers were acquainted with a fair percentage of the songs. And many of the children heard and sang them not only at home but also in the cars en route to and from school.

There were frequent reminders of both adult and child enjoyment. Mrs. Stant would telephone: "Sandra brought home half a new song today. Can you give me the other half? We want to sing it all." Mrs. Weinig would ask with polite impatience: "Where are my new song sheets? Bill's father wants them." Mrs. Irving would telephone excitedly: "*John Henry* was just sung on the radio. It's a grand song; I'm glad you told us the story of it." Mrs. Jones would report: "Peter broke into *John Henry* fortissimo while he was playing today and sang it clear through—I thought you'd like to know." Mrs. Horne would report: "Raymond won't stop singing *Mary Wore Her Red Dress* until we've clothed all our family and friends and distant acquaintances." Mrs. Fairley would tell how that word "patterroller" had tickled Will's sense of humor and how he went all over the house repeating it and chuckling. I would hear about Jane Irving running up and down the playground bank shouting, "Who moan for me"; about Ann pounding clay with solid satisfaction, chanting, "Juba this and Juba that"; about Janet Gleysteen, "hanging out the linen clothes" each evening in her bath, singing all seven stanzas with washcloth as stage property.

I would hear: "These songs are fresh. We like them. At first we thought some of them a little queer, but now we feel at home with them. And we like them."

The music meetings developed into what one of our visitors called a spontaneous laboratory. A number of questions arose, with the new songs as springboards. They were freely—sometimes hotly—discussed.

One of these concerned dialect pronunciation. Shall we sing "dat" or "that," "de" or "the," in songs which, like *Who Dat Tappin' at de Window*, have been set down by the folklore collector in dialect spelling? Aside from the question as to how consistent various collectors are in the recording of dialect—how important to the song is the pronunciation of the words? What sorts of changes can be allowed without loss of character to the song and without loss to the child of a valuable social and speech experience? Or is this experience valuable? And where shall we draw the line between such expressions as "ain't"— imagine correcting it to "aren't" in *My Horses Ain't Hungry*—and "gwine"—which has come to have undemocratic associations of questionable value? Does the use of such stylized expressions as "de," "dat," "gwine"—especially by the educated city singer, to whom they are not natural modes of expression and to whom they signify lower levels of education than his own—tend to be self-conscious, condescending, precious, "cute"? Shall we perhaps just decide to sing the song in a way natural to each of us—not too carefully or precisely—dropping a few final "g's" from the "ings" when the mood strikes us, but not straining after the picturesque?

More extended was the discussion called forth at a music meeting by the song *Juba*, who "killed a yellow cat" with apparent detachment. Several mothers were seriously concerned. They said: "We are trying to teach our children kindness to animals—why, then, a song about killing?" Someone wanted Juba to chase the cat rather than kill it—and from someone else came the rejoinder that children are more apt to chase than to kill anyway, and that to sing about chasing might therefore be worse because it is more likely to be carried out!

16

From this whimsical beginning arose a number of more serious basic considerations. Should we try to shield the child from feeling of sadness, of hurting or being hurt, of killing, dying? *Can* we shield him? Such feelings are not unnatural to him; he has them, to a greater or lesser extent, already within himself. It is not unnatural for a child to build fantasies around killing, hurting, destroying even things or people he loves. If he can sing about these things—can take action through song—the deed is done (in fantasy) and the pressure relieved. Can we not say, then, that having songs around which sing of these things may be a means of easing such feelings within himself, and of helping to make him more comfortable with himself as well as with what is around him?

Further, how much of a sense of sadness or cruelty or destruction does the child extract from mention of these concepts in song? A strong contributing factor is the mood of the music itself, considered as a thing apart from the words of the song. In most fine-art ("classical") song-writing the composer seeks a one-to-one relation between the mood of the words and the mood of the music, thus tipping the scales considerably in either one direction or the other. Folk song, on the other hand, usually maintains an enviable emotional balance. A song of tragedy is often sung to a simple, direct tune—and, as often, to a vivacious one. Songs whose words might be considered painful may make the feet want to dance.

The mood of a song depends to a great extent, of course, on the *manner of singing*—and on the manner of singing will depend to a great extent the child's reaction to the actual words of the song. Do we not too often tend to suggest to the child through manner of singing—and even more through manner of speaking or telling a story—what we think the child *ought* to feel? If a song is sung in a simple straightforward manner, without sentimentality, may we not say that whatever concepts it conveys will either be accepted as a part of the pattern of living—often constituting a valuable extension of the child's experience —or passed on like many other mysteries, to be understood later?

This fear of hurting the child through song-content came to me at that time as somewhat of a surprise. I had no ready-made thought-out answers. I could answer that it had seemed to us—to my husband and myself—a natural thing to sing to our children about all sorts of living, and that you cannot separate living and dying. I could say that we had never laid undue stress on songs of "sadness," but that when they came along we passed some of them on to our children as part of what it was our privilege to give them. I could tell how Peggy, when she was two and a half and in the hospital with an infected burn—not allowed to see anyone but nurses and doctors—had sent down the hospital corridors hour after hour, in a clear high voice, the long story of

Barbara Allen, sung to her and Michael during previous months by their father with other ballads night after night by request. I could point to the rollicking story of the old gray mare as a favorite with our children—the old gray mare who lay down in the creek bed and died, contributing her skin through subsequent stanzas to cutting, curing, and shoemaking "to keep my toes from the winter frost." I could point to John Henry's fatal race with the steam drill as another favorite—the graveyard stanza sometimes sung, sometimes omitted. I could speak of other songs covering varying degrees and sorts of feeling: the regretful prison lament with the haunting tune seeming never to end (*I Been a Bad Bad Girl*) and the song of the whaling boat that never returned because the whale "made a flunder with his tale" (*The Whale Get Strike*) and the lilting Bahaman ditty with the taunting line "I'm going to pack up your eyes with sand." And I could quote from a song most loved by our children—the song of the faithful possum-hunting dog, *Old Blue:*

9. *When old Blue died he died so hard*
    He shook the ground in my back yard.

10. *Old Blue died, I laid him in the shade,*
    I dug his grave with a silver spade.

11. *I let him down with a golden chain,*
    Link by link slipped through my hand.

12. *There is only one thing that bothers my mind,*
    Blue went to heaven, left me behind.

13. *When I get there, first thing I'll do,*
    Grab me a horn and blow for old Blue.

When children grow older and read of murders and dying and killing in our outspoken newspapers, will they perhaps remember such a burial scene as that of old Blue? And who can say that Peggy, wondering why her father and mother never came to see her through long seven days, found some indefinable connection between her own hurt and whatever of the hurt she may have felt or drawn from the words and spirit of the song of Barbara Allen? If a child's unexpected hurts can become connected with hurts he has heard about in story or poetry or song—if he can reach back into his experience and tie these individual hurts of his to what one might call group hurts—will he perhaps feel in his own less lonely?

A subject of still more lively and frequent argument was that of concrete meaning. Must all words and phrases of a song be brought within the child's experience? Should they all be capable of conveying concrete meaning to him? In adapting a song to particular uses must there always exist a direct one-to-one relation between the text of the song and the use to which it is being put? Shall we change the phrase "Who moan for me" to "Who'll go with me" just because "who moan" is outside the word-meaning world of these particular children? How about the lure of *unknown* meaning? As I think of two-year-old Penelope, I think of two characteristic gestures. With one hand she is holding a ball or some concrete object she knows about. With the other she is reaching out, fingers spread wide. To Sarah or to me? Not always. Maybe to a bright ball shining through dark leaves of trees at night, or to a sound up in the sky, or to some even less definite something.

And what do we mean by meaning? How about sound-meaning and touch-meaning? The ears and tongue and lips also test words. And those four repetitions of the refrain of *Riding in the Buggy, Miss Mary Jane*—

> *Who moan for me,*
> *Who moan for me,*
> *Who moan for me, my darling,*
> *Who moan for me?*

—always bear a lusty quality when the children sing them, as though twice as many are singing—singing because they can't help singing—singing as though they are tasting the words and finding them as good and solid as a bar of chocolate.

Again and again this discussion was revived by new songs and new uses for songs. *Do, Do, Pity My Case* is given its first singing at a music meeting. Queries one mother: "What can this mean to my child?" Soon after that one of our three-year-olds, who has been singing little either at home or at school, is reported chanting the phrase all day with exceptional relish. And later on the mother who questioned its usefulness names the "Do Do" song in her monthly music report as her child's current favorite.

And Johnny is counting his buttons while we sing—

> *By'm bye*
> *By'm bye*
> *Stars shining*
> *Number, number one,*
> *Number two, number three—*

Surely we need not change "stars" to "buttons" as we sing and count? Why not give the stars and the buttons a chance to play around together? To be bound too closely to the literal—to a hard and fast relation between the song and a particular use of it—is to cramp the imagination of *both child and adult*.

These discussions never reached, during that year or following years, any official conclusion. But in the minds of some of us they crystallized into a general attitude toward the songs and their uses with children. Yes—improvise on the words of the songs, bring them at times completely into the world the children know. But keep alive, too, the traditional words. Remember that apparently meaningless phrases may mean a great deal to the child in abstract sound experience, besides possessing the value of extending his horizon. Strive to maintain a balance between two of the outstanding values which music like this possesses for him—the vigorous beauty of the traditional text, and an inherent fluidity and creative aliveness which invites improvisation as a natural development in the life of the song.

Why American Folk Music for Our Children?

This kind of traditional or folk music is thoroughly identified with the kind of people who made America as we know it. It is a music they liked and still like. They made it and are still making it. Some of it came with them from other countries and has been little changed. Some of it came with them from other countries and has been much changed. Some of it grew here. All of it has partaken of the making of America. Our children have a right to be brought up with it.

If it is one of the aims of education to induct the child into the realities of the culture in which he will live, may we not say that this traditional music and language and ideology, which has not only grown out of but has in turn influenced that culture—and is still influencing and being used by it—should occupy a familiar place in the child's daily life, even though it may not be current in the particular neighborhood in which he happens to be living. Many of us open a savings account at the bank when a child is born, and add layer after layer of small deposits which he can later draw on for a college education. Perhaps a fund of songs might be begun as early, and added to layer after layer—an ever-growing wealth of materials which he can draw on at will and can take along with him as links from himself to the various aspects of the culture he will be going out to meet.

This music has been a natural part of work, play, sleep, fun, ridicule, love, death. It has grown out of and passed through many ways of living and doing. Facts and fantasies cling to it from its wandering. It knows and tells what people have thought about the ways of living and the things that happened. Through it one can grow in intimate appreciation of the railroads it helped build, the cotton it helped pick, the ships it helped sail, the land-stretches it made less lonely.

Over a period of months several groups of four-year-olds came close in their own way to the growth of railroading, from the laying of tracks (singing *This Old Hammer*) and the drilling of tunnels (*John Henry*) to the assembling of many sorts of train cars (*The Train Is A-Coming*) and finally to the train in motion, "rumbling through the land" (*Little Black Train*) and arriving at the station (*When the Train Comes Along*). Some mornings all the songs in this little song-story-

*It belongs to our children—
it is an integral part
of their cultural heritage*

*It is a bearer of history
and custom*

21

drama were "acted out" in free rhythmic play; sometimes one or two song-plays were enough. The entire song sequence grew spontaneously, day by day, out of the singing of a work song to which the children liked to hammer, fist-to-fist.

It gives early experience of democratic attitudes and values

This kind of music has crossed and recrossed many sorts of boundaries and is still crossing and recrossing them. It can give the children a glimpse of ways of life and thought different from their own. It can do this in an unself-conscious way—not as a teacher who comes especially to instruct, but as a traveler dropping by with stories to tell about places he has come from, and with plans, perhaps, about places to which he may be going.

It has grown through being needed and used— it has adapted itself frequently to new surroundings

This music bears many fingermarks. It has been handled roughly and gently. It has been used. It has been sung and resung—molded, modified by generations of singers from Maine to Florida and across the country. Some songs have acquired hundreds of stanzas.

This adaptability and breadth of experience give it special appeal and value to small children. One song can cover a gamut of experiences. New words can grow out of new needs and uses—and the song can come to be an integral part of a child's living. It can be the window through which children look at themselves, their neighbors, their toys, thoughts. The creative process involved in improvising on the pattern of such a song may not be far removed from that involved in making songs of their own.

When this book was about to go to press I came across a paragraph in an old folklore journal which expressed so intimately the spirit which I had drawn from daily use of the songs with children that it seemed as though the words had come straight out of my own experience. In fact, several of the phrases were almost identical with phrases of my own —phrases which I had mulled over and pulled out of singing and growing and living with the songs over a period of years. This paragraph, written by Natalie Taylor Carlisle and published in Volume V of the Publications of the Texas Folk Lore Society, seems to me significant enough for quotation here:

. . . The subject matter of the old time . . . song was a part of his (the singer's) daily experience. Furthermore, his peculiar style of music was part and parcel of himself. Whatever he experienced, he sang. Most of his songs had few words because most of them centered upon a single idea or circumstance. However, the song itself might be as long as the individual singer wished to make it, depending entirely upon the mood and occupation of the singer and not upon the number

of words in it. Sometimes a song was an entire day's length. The following, a great favorite in past times, is said to have had its origin in a path along a riverside where there were both sand and clay-mud. In walking along this path, which led from plantation quarters to a church, the church people constantly warned each other to keep out of the mud and to stay in the sand. From this warning grew the song:

Take 'em out the mud, Keep your foot in the sand.

After being sung in this order for a long time, the song used to be reversed and sung thus:

> Keep it in the sand,
> Take your foot out the mud.

. . . Thus a song of very few words might become very very long.

Songs like these are not finished in the sense that a piece of fine-art ("classical") music, or even popular music, is finished. They are always ready to grow. They are forever changing, adapting themselves to meet new situations and needs. The traditional singer seldom hands on a song just as he found it: in some way, small or great, he makes the song his own. A single word may change: the soldier's wife and children-twice-three are moved from London to Columbus, or a frog goes courting with a six-shooter instead of sword and pistol. The singer may change many words, or add entire stanzas, or make subtle differences in the tune. Usually such improvisation is spontaneous—the result of mixing a particular person or group, a particular song and a particular occasion or mood.

It is not "finished" or crystallized— it invites improvisation and creative aliveness

No doubt the rhythmic vitality of this music lends ease to the process of improvisation. It gives a basis, a solid structure on which to build. It gives also an impulse to rhythmic activity. Three fourths of the songs in this book are singing games, play-party songs, square-dance tunes, work songs, patting or jigging songs. They are accustomed to action, to being danced to, clapped to, skipped to, worked to. Children listening often start clapping of their own accord, or skipping, or jumping, or kicking their feet, or trying some new motion.

It has rhythmic vitality— it is music of motion

*It is a kind of music
which everyone
can help make—
it invites participation*

It is within the singing capacity of practically everyone—even small children—yet it is "good" music. It is not a music to be worshiped from afar and performed only by those with special gifts or intensively acquired technique—yet it partakes of the quality of greatness. To enjoy it, one need not dress up either oneself or one's voice. One can sit down with it comfortably, knowing that many parents and children have sat down with it before and tested its goodness—knowing that its value as good music has been democratically determined by general agreement and group acceptance.

*It is not just
children's music—
it is family music*

We have said that this music belongs to our children. Perhaps it is even more important to say that it belongs to them as adults. This is not music which they will have to outgrow. It is not a specially prepared baby food, strained and predigested, and administered with an almost unavoidable element of condescension by adults and older brothers and sisters. It need not be discarded along with the kiddy car and the tricycle. Songs like these are sung by all ages. They are family stuff. Fletcher Collins, in his introduction to *Alamance Play-Party Songs and Singing Games*, speaks with conviction:

My own experience, and that of collaborating teachers . . . has been that few (such) songs and dances are ever the exclusive property of one age-group, but rather that as the performer's age increases, so also does the range of his appreciation of such songs. And that is, after all, the prime test of a permanent cultural possession, that it means something progressively to every age-level in every country . . .

These songs glorify the family as the prime social unit, for they have been raised through many centuries of family life, when everyone from grandfather down to the youngest toddler joined in King William was King George's son.

Singing the Songs

So often comes from parents the wistful remark: I like music but I can't sing. The speaker usually means one of two things: either he cannot sing the type of music which he has been taught to look up to as good music (fine-art or "classical" music like that of Bach, Beethoven, Schubert, Brahms, Debussy); or he cannot use his voice in the *manner* of singing which is considered good in performing this type of music. And so, feeling that active participation in good music is beyond him, he hides his voice away and says he cannot sing.

Almost a first requisite in singing with small children is the natural and wholehearted pleasure which the singer finds in the song. *It is the song which is important,* to both singer and listener. And often an "untrained" voice (untrained in *bel canto* singing) will convey to the child a greater enjoyment of the song itself than will the voice which has been made to concentrate hour after hour on the manner of singing the song—on the smoothing-out and perfecting of its own quality.

A first requisite to the traditional (folk) singer too, and to his listeners, is this wholehearted pleasure in the song. Here again it is the song itself which is most important. The writings of folklorists and collectors, and the many phonograph recordings of traditional singers, give constant evidence of this. Vance Randolph, for instance, who has listened to hundreds of Missouri singers and recorded their songs, remarks, in his *Ozark Folksongs,* that "there is a singular absence of affectation or self-consciousness about the Ozark minstrel's performance, and in applauding him one says simply, 'That sure is a good song,' without any mention of the singer's talent or ability."

So allow yourself pleasure in the song, and sing it for its own sake. This is music which anyone can sing and feel he has a right to be comfortable with. And do not have contempt for your voice if it is reedy or breathy or splintery or nasal. Remember that some of the finest traditional singers have similar qualities of voice, and that the songs not only are at home with voices like these, they sound well with them.

Sing the songs simply. Do not feel that you must sing "with expression"—that you must slow down when the song is sad and speed up when it is happy, or that you must vary the dynamics (get loud or soft) according to the meaning of the words. And when you get to the end of a song, feel free to "just stop," without the slowing-down which is so customary in fine-art music.

Sing most of the songs with strong accent on the first of the measure. Feel the beat of the song—its pulse—as a thing which continues throughout the singing of all stanzas or repetitions of the song. In $\frac{2}{4}$ meter, for instance, the quarter note is the beat, or pulse; in $\frac{2}{2}$, the half note is the pulse—and so on. If you want to tap the beat with your foot, feel free to do so, even though fine-art musicians frown on such a practice. On one recording made at a folk festival, the singer's foot-tapping recorded so loud that the singing could scarcely be heard!

Remember that most of the songs are used to being sung at a fairly fast speed. As an aid in determining this speed, precise tempo marks have been added to the general speed indications given in the upper left-hand corner of each song. These tempo marks have been given in terms of the metronome— ♩. = 42, ♩ = 60, et cetera. If you have no metronome, the second-hand of your watch can be of help. Thus, ♩ = 60 means that there are sixty quarter notes within the space of each minute. Try to "get the feel" of the pulse in the ♩ = 60 speed— and then relate other speeds to it. A speed of ♩ = 120 will, for instance, be twice as fast. Do not, however, take these tempo marks too literally. They are only a guide to the speed, and so to the spirit, of the song.

Since a singer can destroy the spirit of naturalness through straining after tones which are too high, most of the songs have been set within a pitch range which is conducive to easy, unforced singing for both adult amateur singers and for children (from middle C to the D a ninth above it). In songs of wider range it has seemed better to give preference to the lower register. Do not be concerned if some tones are low for your voice. Traditional singers often dismiss such tones in a half-sung, half-spoken manner. A number of songs containing wide range and unusual intervals have been included in the book, with the conviction that it is important for children to hear songs which they may not be expected to sing. Sing these songs naturally yourself—and you may be surprised someday to hear your three- or four-year-old (especially if he does not know you are around) singing them with gusto. This happened in our school with a number of songs like *Every Monday Morning*. Children sometimes catch easily intervals and rhythms which to us seem strange or difficult.

Do not feel that you must be able to play the piano in order to enjoy singing with children. These songs are used to being sung unaccompanied. This is especially true of singing games and play party songs and, of course, lullabies. In fact, the piano often gives to the tune a sharpness of line, and to the song-experience a finality, which is not fitting to this music. It can even discourage singing. Hearing the tune played so clearly, the singer grows lazy, and lets his ears rather than his voice use the song.

Improvising on the Words

The songs in this book can be enjoyed without reading any suggestions as to using or singing or accompanying them. To those, however, who feel need of help in the folk art of taking a song and making it one's own—yet leaving within the song the essence of its character as a group possession—the following remarks may be of interest. They are suggestions only, not rules.

First become well acquainted with the song as it stands. This means knowing it well enough to sing it without reading the notes. Let the rhythm of the traditional words be something you feel comfortable with. Carry the song around with you, as children do. You will probably find yourself breaking out with it at odd moments, as children do. You may find you are so at home with it that you feel no need to change it.

Let improvisation on the words be as spontaneous as possible. Let it grow out of the moment, the day, the child, and you. Tomorrow something quite different may happen. This is the way many songs like these have grown and changed in the past.

You may be tempted at times to take advantage of the adaptability of a song and twist it in a way unnatural to it. Remember, then, that the changes through which this music has already passed have been gradual, and that improvisation on words has for the most part come from singers brought up with music like it—singers who understood instinctively its nature and habits.

Let improvisation come from the child as much as possible—from things he happens to do or say or sing. Don't hesitate to join in on the fun—but remember that the adult faces numerous pitfalls when "thinking up" words for children, such as affectation or overconscientious attention to particular uses for a song, or preconceived notions as to child speech, understanding, or enjoyment.

Make sure that improvisation of new words does not deprive the child of old traditional words. "This lady she wears a dark green shawl" gives him something quite different in image and sound from the adaptation "This Betsy she wears her light blue dress." Perhaps you might say to him: "This song belongs to many people, and they sing it in different ways." Give the child, too, experience of some of the song titles—as, for instance, the unforgettable *Down by the Greenwood Sidey-o*.

Avoid the feeling that a direct one-to-one relation is essential between the words of a song and the action or use to which it is being momentarily put. It is debatable whether "Let's go hunting" should be changed to "Let's go skipping" just because children are skipping to the music of *Billy Barlow*. There will, of course, be times when the spontaneity of the moment can best be captured through a literal approach. But it should be borne in mind that the integrity and often the beauty of the song-as-a-whole may suffer from too great bondage to the literal.

Remember that the suggested improvisations which accompany many of the songs in this book are given only as springboards. Most of them grew out of some specific moment, motion, word, or wish. With you and your children something quite different may happen.

If, when singing a song like *Mary Wore Her Red Dress*, you ask children what of their own they would like to sing about, you sometimes receive answers which do not fit the rhythm of the song. Traditional singers often insert extra counts to care for such syllables. Children laugh with the pleasure of hearing so many words elbow their way into the middle of a song pattern they know.

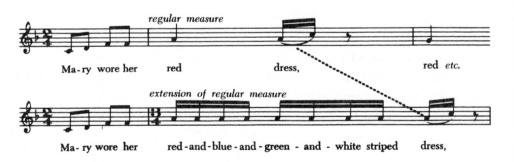

Using the Songs at Home

It is a natural thing to pick up the rhythm of a song and carry it around the house, letting it grow out of or into the varied activities and inactivities that are part of a day. One must be careful, of course, not to draw songs in by the hair of their heads (or the tails of their notes) —nor to feel that every time one goes upstairs or downstairs one must sing a song about it. Singing with small children should be casual and unpretentious. For this reason, homemade songs and chants are often better than songs whose patterns you feel are cut and finished. The rhythm and nuances of children's speaking voices are often half over the border to music, and a chance remark or question will suggest a tune. This occurred one morning in our family with a request urgently repeated:

But you need not feel that the "finished" songs are finished. Feel free to use tidbits of songs you know. These also make excellent tone plays. One evening I happened to sing *By'm Bye* to Penelope as I was putting her to bed. A few evenings later, as I was taking her on her customary rounds, we sang good-by to each of the family bedrooms. There was not time to sing the whole *By'm Bye* song—and it would have seemed artificial. So we sang only the beginning interval and its echo. This soon became a ritual. It extended to an accidental peek out the window at the snow (By'm bye, snow), and the snow still later became rain or stars or moon or birds, according to the moment. One evening we saw her slipping into her sisters' rooms and heard *By'm Bye* being sung to all the dolls and animals in their cradles. She sang that simple interval of a fourth as though in it were contained many intangible things.

This using of pieces of songs you know—small motives, or half phrases or phrases—is an excellent springboard toward the making of your own songs. One sure-fire way of getting children upstairs is to sing about it. Start the song *Such a Getting Upstairs,* and the process is accomplished quickly. But at times the singing-through of a complete song at the "appropriate" moment seems too formal and planned, as though the stage had been set in advance. Try, then, letting your voice play around with just part of the song: let it wander off and travel along the path of similar rhythms on different (or the same) pitch levels. Perhaps you will find yourself making variations on the basic motive—but do not think too hard about trying to make a "good tune." The rhythm and spontaneity are more important at first. Your beginning might happen something like this:

The song need not have a formal end—it can just stop.

Many work songs consist chiefly of a small motive repeated over and over, picked up and carried along, sometimes by one person, sometimes by another, to the rhythm of tie-tamping on the railroad, or log chopping or rock splitting. Not unrelated were some of the song experiences which Barbara and I had as we walked a lonely half-mile stretch from school, throwing song phrases back and forth—sometimes our own, sometimes improvisations on songs we knew. And one day when the family was playing Flinch, Peggy drew a Number 1 from the card stack and half sang, half chanted in triumph as she continued to build up the pile of cards:

The rhythm caught and stuck. For months we never played the game without it.

There are times, of course, when entire songs—even extensions of them—fit the pattern of the day informally and without artificiality. Most mothers find some pleasant way of pulling shirts over children's heads. We happened on one, to the tune of *Where, Oh, Where, Is Pretty Little Susie?*

> *Where oh where is pretty little Penny,*
> *Where oh where is pretty little Penny,*
> *Where oh where is pretty little Penny,*
> *'Way down yonder in the polo shirt.*
>
> *Come on, girls, let's go find her,*
> *Come on, girls, let's go find her,*
> *Come on, girls, let's go find her,*
> *'Way down yonder in the polo shirt.*

And the children did seem to dress faster when we added, stanza by stanza, minute details about *John the Rabbit's* habits of dressing. And was it partly the unendingness of *Mary Had a Baby* which quieted a sick child day after day? It usually began:

> *Mammy had a baby, aye Lord,*
> *Mammy had a baby, aye my Lord,*
> *Mammy had a baby, aye Lord,*
> *The people keep a-coming and the train done gone.*
>
> *Baby named Ronnie, aye Lord,*
> *Baby named Ronnie, aye Lord,*
> *Baby named Ronnie, aye Lord,*
> *The people keep a-coming and the train done gone.*
>
> *Baby had blue eyes, aye Lord, etc.*

—but from then on the song was never twice the same.

There is always bedtime. Song singing has one advantage over story reading: the room can be dark, inviting sleep. And darkness, in turn, through depriving the singer of a book to rely on, can encourage the spontaneous making of new stanzas. As to choice of songs, you may find lively ones as quieting as quiet ones. Every night Michael wanted *Turtle Dove* before the door was closed to its inch of crack—but there had usually been a spirited singing session preceding it. And the fast crisp tune of the old minstrel song *Buffalo Girls* lays Penelope's head quiet on the pillow to hear Peggy and Barbara improvise questions-and-answers on any or all of the day's happenings, from dancing by the light of the sun to milk-drinking to tooth-brushing to looking at the stars, and on, until the song sends them one by one away to bed.

Buf-fa-lo girls ain't you com-ing out to-night,   com-ing out to-night, com-ing out to-night,

Buf - fa-lo girls, ain't you com-ing out to-night, to   dance by the light of the moon?

Ain't you, ain't you, ain't you, ain't you com-ing out to-night, com-ing out to-night, com-ing out to-night,

Ain't you, ain't you, ain't you, ain't you com-ing out to-night, to dance by the light of the moon?

Certainly music like this is not typical "quiet music." Neither are courting songs like *Cindy*, nor dance songs like *Cripple Creek*, nor spirituals like *Them Bones*, nor ballads like *Black Jack Davy*, nor work songs like *John Henry*, nor song-chants like *John Done Saw That Number*, with such lines as these:

> *God told the angel:*
> *Go down, see 'bout old John.*
> *Angel flew from the bottom of the pit,*
> *Gathered the sun all in her fist,*
> *Gathered the moon all 'round her wrist,*
> *Gathered the stars all under her feet,*
> *Gathered the wind all 'round her waist,*
>
> *Crying Holy, Lord,*
> *Crying Holy, Lord,*
> *Crying Holy, Lord,*
> *Crying Holy.*

You yourself, through singing and using, will find sorts of songs which you and your own children like to sing. It might be of interest to recall the frequent reference in folklore books to ballads of outlawry, sadness, death, even murder, as "a song my mother used to sing me to sleep with."

Using the Songs at School

One thing which impressed me when I started singing and playing with groups of small children was the importance of different sorts of links.

First there was the link between the children and me. To be sure, I had plenty of songs knocking around in my head. But somehow these songs had to meet and get acquainted with embryo songs in the children's heads, and with rhythms knocking around in their feet and arms and bodies. Thus each song-and-action session with the children must be a joint creation of theirs and mine. We were making a sort of musical composition together, in which one song experience grew out of another, and out of that another, and so on.

Sometimes this flow came easy. Sometimes it was hard to follow. Sometimes links had to be searched for—not only links between the children and me but, this time, links from one song to another, or occasionally from one word or motion to another.

Certain songs began to slip into these gaps as link songs. They were usually, I realized later, of the dance or play-party type, like *Old Joe Clarke* or *Jim Along Josie*—songs which were used to being thrown around, played with, joked with. One of these had several hundred stanzas already. No wonder such songs could make us feel at home with ourselves and with each other: they were seasoned travelers. Songs like these could easily take on the color and spirit of any situation. They could, like *Toodala*, keep growing from day to day, become the warp on which the fabric of an entire morning's thoughts and actions and wishes might be woven.

I came to feel that the children's gain, and mine, from such experiences was not just a piece of music—a song. Greater gain was the feeling we had of making something together, of taking a small piece of experience and using it—sometimes just letting it grow, sometimes nurturing it. Such experiencing of a combined individual and group accomplishment can mean a great deal to the individual taking part in it. He has not only made a contribution: he receives a contribution from the group in return. And perhaps here was the most important link of all—the link created from the individual to the group, and vice versa.

Important to the adult guiding such a process of give-and-take is the question of balance, the decision when to follow the child and when to lead. For continuity, one of the basic elements in a creative process, can be lost through lack of selectiveness. In the middle of singing *Hush, Little Baby,* Renny's heels get busy in a fast rhythm-beat on the floor. It is hard to decide whether to complete the experience already begun or to follow Renny on to another. A favorite heel-tapping rhythm play grew from following through just such a "diversion of attention." At the end of an extended session of quiet shoe-tying to the refrain of *Lula Gal,* the stanza was begun—and somebody's feet began kicking up and down. The joyful exhilaration which rose with the layers of noise added by each pair of shoes as it joined the others, made the diversion seem right—a healthy and natural release. So we went on and on with the music, returning finally to the quiet refrain—for the fun of more kicking again. Such a decision may depend on many factors—among them, the diverter's normal attention span. For if he is a habitual interrupter and can be counted on to desert the next activity as soon as it is begun, it is questionable whether his impulse is significant to the group or to himself. Perhaps most of all you will be listening for the group's reaction to the "interruption." Jock jumped up one day while we were singing a quiet song and started turning around and around. We went on singing our quiet song. Barry jumped up to join Jock. We still went on singing. Louis and Lucia jumped up too—and we switched to "Round and round, old Joe Clarke," continuing the lively rhythm of this favorite song by group insistence through many repetitions.

"Adverse" situations or environment can often be used as springboards to new experiences. In one school there were four steps leading to a forbidden area. Adventure always seemed up those steps. With a song about "such a getting upstairs"—which involved stopping at the top and waiting until everyone was ready to sing about "such a gettin' downstairs"—the steps could be enjoyed. Then too there was David, who started pulling Peter's hair. It seemed a natural thing to remember the lines from an old ballad:

> *Brother, comb my sweetheart's hair*
> *As we go marching home.*

As we sang the song over and over, David switched from pulling to combing. Soon everyone was busy combing someone's hair, and another finger play had been "discovered" by the group for itself.

While working with groups of children at various schools over a period of several years, I have from time to time jotted down tentative conclusions as reminders to myself and as possible help to others. They are the product of concrete daily experience with the type of songs contained in this book, but may be found to have general value.

Sing the song first at its natural speed—not too slowly, precisely or carefully. The first singing should give the spirit of the song, an impression of the song as a whole rather than an analysis of it. When a song has only one stanza, sing it over and over, not just once, so that the child not only meets the song but gets a little acquainted before it is gone.

Songs like these should not drag. Remember that most of them are accustomed to a lively speed and a strong metrical accent (on the first beat of each measure). This should be especially borne in mind when using them for rhythmic play.

Sit with the children on the floor when you can, especially with two- and three-year-olds. Getting closer together occasionally can give both adult and children greater confidence. Some "difficult moments" have automatically disappeared when the adult came down off the piano stool.

Do not be concerned if small children do not sing when part of a group. Reports gathered from mothers have frequently shown that children who are not participating at school are singing with gusto at home. Perhaps they may like to tap their feet or clap their hands while others sing. But do not be disturbed if they "just sit." One never knows what they are taking in or when they will start singing.

Longer songs may be simplified at first for smaller children by omitting the words of a refrain (as in *All Around the Kitchen*) or of a stanza (as in *Run, Chillen, Run*). The music of that section may perhaps be played without singing, as an instrumental interlude.

Many of these songs make excellent rhythm band music, especially songs of the dance or play-party type like *Old Joe Clarke, Skip-a to My Lou, Jingle at the Window,* and others. A list of such songs is given in the classified index.

Keep-going-ness is one of the notable characteristics in traditional performance of music like this. Do not hesitate, especially when using the songs for rhythmic activity, to keep the music going through many repetitions—sometimes with singing, sometimes without. Do not fear monotony: it is a valuable quality.

Although most groups of children want and probably need more action songs than "listening" songs, bear in mind too the value of the quiet song, and seek each day what seems the best balance for that day between the two types. The changing needs and moods of the children will be your guide on each occasion. Be ready with quiet music if you see unconstructive wildness growing out of too much activity—but do not force a quiet song just for the sake of variety.

Do not be in a hurry to move from one song or activity to another. Children occasionally derive more pleasure and value from one or two songs or activities which they like than from a variety of half-tasted experiences. One morning a group of children became so enamored of turning around and around to *Old Joe Clarke* that they wanted to do nothing else, and greeted each tentative departure to another song with clamors for return to this momentary favorite. We spent most of a music period turning around and around, one way and another.

It is especially important to feel unhurried with the smallest children. A two-year-old who stands by unmoving through three or four repetitions of a song may be just ready to discover his own way of meeting and enjoying the music during a fifth or sixth repetition. Be patient and wait and watch while the music does the urging—then still be patient and continue the music long enough to allow the children full satisfaction in their discovery before leading on to another.

In singing a new song for the first time to a group of children you will occasionally feel hesitant—even anxious—because you are uncertain of their reaction to it. At such times you may find yourself hurrying on too soon to a well-tried song which you and the children together know better. Try instead, sometimes, keeping the new song going, giving the children plenty of time to become familiar with it, singing it on and on in one uninterrupted song experience—like a train going past station after station rather than a trolley stopping at each street corner. Often a song begun with inner uncertainty but kept going in this way has seemed to gather momentum as it went along, increasing not in speed but in a sense of conviction within both adult and children.

If there is a group teacher, and she remains in the room with the children during the music period, rely on her as little as possible for group control. Establish an understanding with her as to her role and as to your policy and manner of procedure, and ask that she give help only as a last resort (either in control or suggestion or stimulus)—and perhaps only on some predetermined sign from you. And lean on her only when a child's persistent diversion of group attention has proven unusable creatively and destructive of group enjoyment. On a number of occasions a creative moment has been almost lost through overzealous adult attempt to control the attention of everyone in the group. "Now you must all listen to the music"—and the nursery becomes a concert hall.

Have confidence, then, in yourself and the child. Remember that, through fear of losing control of a group, you may also lose what might have been a productive experience. Be ready with a few "link" songs which can always be counted on to draw the children together in case of "emergency"—and then feel free to welcome the unexpected and to follow where it leads.

If a child gets up and leaves a singing group, the adult's first thought may be that he has lost interest and will be a disturbance to others, and that he should therefore either be called back to the group or asked to leave the room. Yet that child at that moment may be finding his way of living-through what the song means for him.

When Carter got up during the first singing of *When the Train Comes Along*—

> *If my mother ask for me*
> *If my mother ask for me*
> *I'm going to meet her at the station*
> *When the train comes along*—

it was not clear whether he had lost interest and was wandering off to some other activity. His actions were vague, he sauntered a roundabout way hither and yon in apparently lackadaisical fashion. The group watched him while we went on singing, but nobody joined him. I was uncertain whether to continue the new song or to drop it and return to it another day. But we kept our eyes on Carter and went on singing the stanza over and over—

> *If my mother ask for me*
> *If my mother ask for me*——

After a while Carter paused over by the door, went through a few mysterious motions, then came a straight way back to the group and sat down. "I met my mother at the station," he explained.

Listen to the child, then, and wait and watch and be ready for him without hurry—and think occasionally of that perky phrase from the Bahaman song—

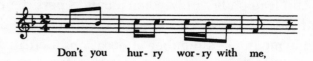

And give to the child, rather than to the piano, your eyes and attention. Remember that the smallest movement of his fingers may be a thread to follow—a link from one song to the next, or from him to you, or from him to the group—and so from the group back to him again.

Tone Play and Phrase Repetition

Children who are shy about singing (and many of them are, especially when they think someone is listening) will sometimes join in on a single tone when they would not think of tackling a whole row of them. This single tone is a thing they can identify and pin to—somewhat as, in a street of row-houses all alike, they might feel comforted to see a flag flying from their own window.

Use of tone-play should be as spontaneous as possible. Folk songs, especially of the work-song or "response" type, provide made-to-order tone-plays. The single-tone response is, of course, the simplest. Children join in on the "yes ma'am's" of *Did You Go to the Barney?* or *Oh, John the Rabbit* without invitation, and long before they sing the whole song.

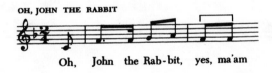

A final tone, as in *Down Came a Lady,* or a repeated initial tone, as in *Oh, Oh, the Sunshine,* also provides natural tone-play material.

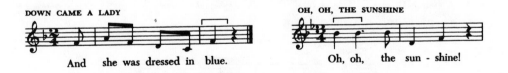

Two-tone tone-play is only a little less simple. The echoed interval of a fourth in *By'm Bye* is easy to sing.

Nonsense refrains are time-honored tone-plays. *The Little Pig* contains one of the simplest. *Bought Me a Cat* presents a wide variety.

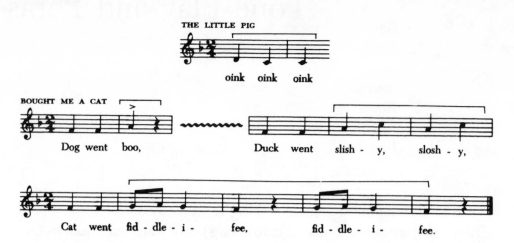

THE LITTLE PIG

oink   oink   oink

BOUGHT ME A CAT

Dog went   boo,   Duck   went   slish - y,   slosh - y,

Cat went   fid - dle - i -   fee,   fid - dle - i -   fee.

Songs like *There Was a Man and He Was Mad* and *Hush, Little Baby* invite children to supply rhyming words at the end of the stanza—and tones as well.

THERE WAS A MAN

pud- ding bag.

HUSH, LITTLE BABY

mock- ing bird.

Responses at different pitch levels within the same song, as in *I Got a Letter, Miss Julie Ann Johnson,* and *The Train Is A-Coming,* make slightly more advanced tone-plays.

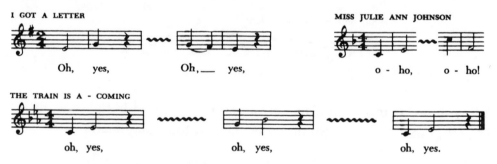

I GOT A LETTER

Oh,   yes,   Oh,___ yes,

MISS JULIE ANN JOHNSON

o - ho,   o - ho!

THE TRAIN IS A - COMING

oh, yes,   oh, yes,   oh, yes.

And even small children purse their lips to make a try at whistling the refrain of *Have a Little Dog*.

HAVE A LITTLE DOG

(Whistle_____)

A sort of extended tone-play occurs when the singer for one reason or another repeats a phrase or part of a phrase within the fabric of a song. Such repetition gives the child more to hold on to in getting acquainted with the song than does the shorter tone-play. It also adds a feeling of elasticity to the singing experience, even approaching at times the nature of the creative process, though no new music or words be added. Often too, it seems, through its very monotony and stubborn repetition of beat, to increase the impulse to rhythmic motion.

Round and round
(And round and round
And round and round
And round and round), old Joe Clarke,
Round and round I say,
Round and round, old Joe Clarke,
I ain't got long to stay.

The number of repetitions of such key phrases is never twice the same. It follows the children's individual needs and reactions. Slow or shy children may require the encouragement of many repetitions before joining the others in turning around or scraping up sand.

Scraping up sand
(And scraping up sand
And scraping up sand
And scraping up sand
And scraping up sand
And scraping up sand
And scraping up sand) in the bottom of the sea,
Shiloh, shiloh,
Scraping up sand in the bottom of the sea,
Shiloh, Liza Jane.

There may be two shoes to tie today, and ten tomorrow.

Lula gal, Lula gal,
Lula gal, Lula gal,
Tie my shoe, boy, tie my shoe,
Tie my shoe, boy, tie my shoe,
(Tie my shoe, boy, tie my shoe,
Tie my shoe, boy, tie my shoe).

And there is no telling from day to day how long it will take to hang out the clothes, or bring them in, or mend them.

Twas on a Tuesday morning
The first I saw my darling
A-hanging out the linen clothes,
A-hanging out the linen clothes,
(A-hanging out the linen clothes,
A-hanging out the linen clothes,
A-hanging out the linen clothes).

When singing with larger groups of children, repetition of this sort is also useful as a means of shortening songs which would normally devote an entire stanza or line to each child.

> *Goodbye, Kathy, o-ho!*
> *Goodbye, Jimmy, o-ho!*
> *Goodbye, Richard,*
> *(And Vivian*
> *And Marjory*
> *And Alice*
> *And George*
> *And Sue*
> *And Kiki*
> *And Lynne*
> *And Marna) o-ho!*
> *Goodbye, Abigail, o-ho!*

Accompanying the Songs

These songs do not need any instrumental background. Most of them are used to being sung without accompaniment. When accompanied, the most usual instruments are the guitar, autoharp, mandolin, banjo, accordion, and harmonica. If you can play any of these, use them freely. Since, however, the piano is the instrument most frequently found in town and city homes and schools, the following suggestions are chiefly concerned with this instrument as background to songs and activities for small children, and with its use in as easy and natural a manner as possible.

One trouble with the piano as an accompanying instrument in singing with small children is that the children are more likely to see the pianist's back than his face. Make sure you are giving most of your attention to the child rather than to the piano. If the written accompaniment keeps your eye on the page, abandon it. Try letting the left hand play the tune along with the right, an octave below. Or if playing with two hands keeps your eye on the piano keys, try playing the tune with one hand. Certainly an unaccompanied tune played with convincing and regular rhythmic beat has more meaning than an accompanied tune whose rhythmic outline is blurred through hesitation.

A strongly rhythmic accompaniment can, however, influence noticeably the reaction of a group to a song, especially when the song is used for rhythmic play. It can provide a rhythmic framework for the tune. It can and should emphasize the pulse of the tune. It can give variety in rhythmic experience yet be of simplest harmonic structure.

You may find that "chording" by ear allows you to provide a more natural and rhythmic accompaniment than reading by note, even if you are a fairly good note reader. You may find, too, that chording a tune is easier than you think. Chord letters have been placed above each staff line, as aid not only to players of traditional instruments like the guitar, but also to pianists who want to try making their own accompaniments. These chord letters represent, in all but a few songs, a simplification of the harmonies underlying the written accompaniments.

Look over the songs and see how few chords you need to know. Most songs require only the three common chords or triads of the key in which the song is set. These are built up, in intervals of a 3rd, on the first, fourth, and fifth tones or steps of the scale. The scales most used in this book, and the three common chords of each scale, are given below. The seventh chord (formed by placing another interval of a 3rd on top of a triad) is included for completeness, since a number of chord letters in the songs call for seventh chords. In chording, however, the triad can always be substituted for the seventh if the latter is too difficult to play—G for G^7, D for D^7, etc.

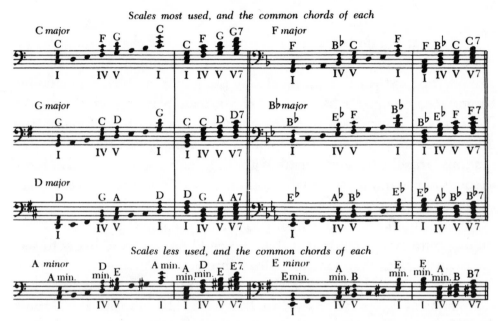

Scales most used, and the common chords of each

Scales less used, and the common chords of each

In the six most used scales there are altogether only eight triads to learn: C, G, D, A, F, B♭, E♭, A♭. Try acquainting your left hand (and your right) with these chords. Play them in a few simple rhythmic patterns until you are so at home with them that you can establish a pattern and keep it going with little or no attention. Think more in terms of motion than of richness. Think of keeping the tune moving along, of giving it legs to walk or run on rather than a plush chair to sit in. If all three tones of a chord sound too "thick" when played close together, try thinning the chord, either by omitting one of the tones, or by changing the position or order of the tones, or by playing the chord-tones separately in any of a number of patterns. Just moving a chord an octave higher sometimes helps. The following example gives a few simple patterns of tone-arrangement possible in the use of any one triad.

C Chord - one tone omitted

C Chord - complete

Do not feel obliged to make frequent change back and forth from one chord to another (C to F, F to C, et cetera). Seek simplicity rather than variety of harmonic structure. Traditional guitar and banjo players are not in a hurry to move from one basic harmony to another. In a song like *Down Came a Lady,* for instance, they would probably stay on the F chord until the next to last measure—and some players would not change chord at all. In *Old Molly Hare* the traditional player would be apt to omit the added IV chord. In *Skip-a to My Lou* and *Billy Barlow,* on the other hand, the chord-tones are clearly outlined by the tune itself. This is true of a great many of these songs.

Sometimes a single song can follow or lead the children through a variety of experiences by means of a few simple changes in type of accompaniment. The accompaniment can be varied in *rhythmic pattern* (for running, walking, skipping, etc.); in *arrangement of tones* (close together, far apart, all high, all low, etc.); in *quality of tone* (smooth, roughly picked, lightly picked, dull and heavy, etc.); in dynamics, or *amount of tone* (loud, soft, medium loud, medium soft, etc.). Sometimes chording by ear makes easier this adapting of types of accompaniment to types of activity—gives the player more freedom to move from one rhythmic pattern to another, allows him to follow more spontaneously when a new mood or motion appears. The variations included with the song *Jim Along Josie* give an idea of the ease with which this can be done. The same basic chords are used throughout the variations. Accompaniments to many other songs can be as easily varied.

Remember, in changing the dynamics from one rhythmic activity to another (soft for tiptoe, loud for jumping, medium loud for walking, hopping, skipping, etc.), not to feel you must vary the loudness or softness *within* any one variation. Do not try to play with "expression" or shading. Play simply. Bring the song into the room in natural straightforward manner, as an old friend with whom you feel comfortable.

Avoid especially, in most songs, a heavy left hand. Chording will usually sound best when played with varying degrees of staccato, or picked, "popcorn" tone—sometimes light, sometimes brittle, sometimes half-staccato, but seldom wooden or plodding. And take care not to play with excessive loudness, unless for particular effect. Older children of seven or eight have come troubled to the piano, saying: "You are playing so loud, I can't hear the words." Younger children seldom voice such helpful reminders.

Remember, too, when playing for rhythmic activity, to give vigorous metrical accent on the first beats of measures—to feel the pulse of the song. And keep the music going; do not stop playing any one song too soon. Repeat it over and over, without pausing between repetitions, for if you pause between you are apt to lose the pulse and the keep-going-ness. Words of songs may be omitted entirely for rhythmic play or may be alternately sung and omitted. Traditional banjo pickers often do this, playing intricate variations on a tune for several minutes, then laying the words of a single stanza on top of the playing, then more playing, then another stanza, and so on ad lib. The banjo does not stop playing, from beginning to end of the performance. There is no break in pulse or continuity.

Explore the wide pitch-span of the piano, low to high. You may be inclined at first to stay safely at home near middle C, since pioneering into the outer octaves draws the hands away from each other. Yet the same song played in various octave combinations can give quite different effects. Get used to playing all over the piano. Try moving a chord or a tune or part of a tune around among the seven octave positions. Take the C chord, for instance, and learn to move it quickly from one octave to the next. Take a tune in the key of C and learn to play it from the same tone of each octave. Then see how many different octave combinations the two hands can find—playing sometimes two octaves apart, or three, or four, or both very high or very low. Over a score of such octave combinations are possible, only a few of which are included among the *Jim Along Josie* variations.

Do not feel you must be prepared with a specific song to match every possible request. When Jock comes up to the piano with his body full of angles, wanting to be a tiger, it would be a shame to postpone his urge because you cannot remember a ready-made tiger song in a hurry. He will be glad to show you his way of being a tiger, and you can make your own tiger music—with your eyes more on Jock than on the piano keys. Perhaps you may establish the beat or pulse of the music with some easy figure in the left hand—the warp of the music you are about to weave. With that continuing, you are free to let the right hand travel in and out among dissonances and consonances, looking sometimes for a tune, sometimes for a rhythm. Do not be afraid of wrong notes. You may find, if you come back again and again to a so-called wrong (or rough) note, that it sounds right—that it "belongs" and you like it. If not, you can try sliding your finger from the rough note to a "smoother" one close by. You may even find yourself experimenting with the sound of adjacent tones (half and whole steps) played simultaneously—and liking them too. Perhaps most important is the feeling that each tone or interval which you play *pulls* to another. Listen for this pull. See if your fingers can get the feel of it without help from your eyes—for Jock and the other tigers who have joined him are vital threads in the musical cloth you are weaving.

Nonsense

One sturdy element has been left out of the preceding chapters. It was left out because it belonged in all of them. It was present at all the music meetings and during the earnest telephone discussions on the meaning of meaning. It is certainly one of the basic values to children in music like this. It should be a live ingredient in the process of improvisation, whether at home or at school, and can even make itself heard in the playing of the music. It is the homely yeast and soda in the process of song mixing—its immediate momentary bubbling will appear artificial only to those who forget how heavy the bread can be without it.

This element is—a sense of humor. An appreciation of nonsense. A willingness to lay logic aside, to respect the ridiculous.

Children like nonsense. They come asking fondly for "that silly old song" (*Old Aunt Kate*). They wait through five stanzas of *The Little Pig* to laugh loud at "the woman, the man, and the little piggee" all lying on the shelf ("on the *shelf!*" they repeat with superior scorn for such foolishness—then ask for the song all over again).

The sense of the funny need not obtrude. One can simply be ready to welcome it when it appears, as an old friend dropping in for a chat rather than as a formally invited guest. The adult must take care, while playing around with songs and having fun with them himself, not to thrust unduly on children his own concepts of nonsense. If he does, he may find himself falling into the snare of being "cute" instead. He should not, on the other hand, always hold back, waiting for the child to take the lead. Part of what he can contribute is the sense of adventure, of discovering something together.

Children often find fun in corners where adults would overlook it. When Tony first heard *She'll Be Coming Round the Mountain When She Comes*, he gave a man-size shout. "She'll be *comin'* when she comes!" he repeated with delight, then turned to include me in his discovery: "That's another foolish one, isn't it!" And would you think of a song like *Hush 'n' Bye* as foolish?

> *Hush 'n' bye, don't you cry,*
> *Go to sleep, you little baby,*
> *When you wake you shall have some cake*
> *And all the pretty little horses.*

Yet, the day after we had sung it for the first time, someone begged for "that new foolish song"—and I floundered until he explained: "You know—the song where the *baby* eats *cake*."

American folklore is, of course, full of rugged humor. The girls poke fun at the boys—

> *Old Dan Tucker was a mighty man,*
> *He washed his face in a frying pan,*
> *Combed his hair with a wagon wheel,*
> *And died with a toothache in his heel.*

—and the boys poke fun at the girls—

> *I went down to Cindy's house,*
> *She was standing in the door,*
> *Her shoes and stockings in her hand*
> *And her feet all over the floor.*

—and fibbing fun is everywhere. Darby's ram has horns that reach up to the moon ("a man went up in January and never got down till June"); the boll weevil cannot be frozen by ice nor burned by fire ("Here I are, here I are, this'll be my home"); the elephant jumps over the fence so high that he clears the sky ("never came back 'til the Fourth of July"). Not so far from the spirit of this is the child who sings about the rain raining all over the piano instead of the grass, or John the Rabbit eating nails and splinters instead of carrots, or the man who was so mad that he jumped into a dog's bark.

THE SONGS

Yonder She Comes

Moderately fast ♩=120

MISSOURI

Yon-der she comes And it's how-dy how-dy do, Oh, where have you been since the last that I met you?

Ending

2. Rise you up, my lady (or gentleman),
Present to me your hand,
I know you are a pretty girl (or handsome man),
The prettiest in the land.

Down Came a Lady

LORD DANIEL'S WIFE

VIRGINIA

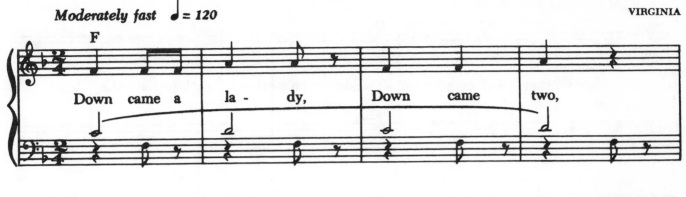

Down came a lady, Down came two, Down came Lord Dan'-l's wife And she was dressed in blue.

IMPROVISATION and RHYTHMIC PLAY: *In one school the steps were steep, and each person's coming down was an event to sing about.*

Down came a lady,
Down came two,
Down came Miss Peggy Smith
And she was dressed in blue.

The lady (or gentleman) may be doing other things—coming in, jumping up, dancing away. Several children may be included in one stanza:

In came Matthew,
Jeremy too,
In came Marianne
And she was dressed in blue.

TONE PLAY:

Adult: And she was dressed in . . .
Child: . . . . blue.

Who's That Tapping at the Window?

Moderately fast ♩=88

VIRGINIA

Who's that tap-ping at the win-dow? Who's that knock-ing at the door?

Mam - my tap-ping at the win-dow, Pap - py knock-ing at the door.

NAME PLAY and FINGER PLAY:

Who's that tapping at the window?
Who's that knocking at the door?
Danny tapping at the window,
Mika knocking at the door.

If there are many children, the music of the last two lines can be extended to include them all. Tapping may be light; knocking, heavy.

Tony tapping at the window,
Gary knocking at the door,
Mora tapping at the window,
Maggie knocking at the door,
and so on.

52

Such a Getting Upstairs

Fast ♩ = 120

Such a get-ting up-stairs I nev-er did see,

Repeat ad lib

Such a get-ting up-stairs it don't suit me.

This is a favorite going-up-to-bed song. It can be a getting-down-stairs song as well. It is the refrain of a play-party tune whose second section can be whistled or hummed or played, or sung with varying words like the following from Virginia:

Some love cof-fee, some love tea, But I love the pret-ty girl that winks at me,

The folklorist Winston Wilkinson notes the similarity of a Virginia version of this tune to that of an old English Morris Dance tune, and points further to the rites of the old processional dance, in which the performers danced down the streets, and into the village houses, and up the stairs and down again.

Toodala

Moderately fast ♩ = 120

G   C   G

Might-y pret-ty mo-tion, too-da-la, too-da-la, too-da-la,

D7   G   Ending

Might-y pret-ty mo-tion, too-da-la, too-da-la-la la-dy.

2. Rock old Soni, toodala, toodala, toodala,
   Rock old Soni, toodala, toodala-la-lady.

3. Right back this way, toodala, toodala, toodala, etc.

4. Swing your partner, toodala, toodala, toodala, etc.

Toodala parties used to be held frequently in Texas. The dancing was usually outdoors; entire families came, from babies to old men, and the young people danced. Words were improvised during the dancing, which was in the manner of square dancing.

IMPROVISATION and RHYTHMIC PLAY: *This dance song sings easily over and over without stopping—picking up whatever things are happening, repeating in unbroken flow words or phrases the children are saying, noticing new toys, bright colors, the weather. For instance:*

(The children are coming in from outdoors, and no child's name is left out of the song)

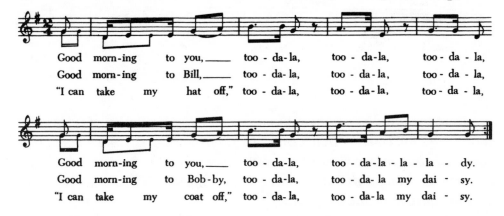

Good morn-ing to you,____ too-da-la, too-da-la, too-da-la,
Good morn-ing to Bill,____ too-da-la, too-da-la, too-da-la,
"I can take my hat off," too-da-la, too-da-la, too-da-la,

Good morn-ing to you,____ too-da-la, too-da-la-la-la-dy.
Good morn-ing to Bob-by, too-da-la, too-da-la my dai-sy.
"I can take my coat off," too-da-la, too-da-la my dai-sy.

54

Good morning to Sam, toodala, toodala, toodala,
He takes his hat off, toodala, toodala my daisy.

Here comes Joanna, toodala, toodala, toodala,
She has her coat on, toodala, toodala my daisy.

She can pull it off now, toodala, toodala, toodala,
She can do it herself, toodala, toodala-la-lady.

(Each laborious detail becomes part of the growing song)

Pulled off my rubbers, toodala, toodala, toodala,
They're hard to pull off, toodala, toodala-la-lady.

Take off my leggings, toodala, toodala, toodala,
Can do it myself, toodala, toodala my daisy.

I unbutton my coat, toodala, toodala, toodala,
I can do it myself, toodala, toodala-la-lady.

Has lots of buttons, toodala, toodala, toodala,
One, two, three, four, five, toodala, toodala-la-lady.

It hangs up high, toodala, toodala, toodala,
Hang it up myself, toodala, toodala my daisy.

(The children gather around one by one, waiting for the song to tell more about what they are doing or saying or hearing or holding in their hands. Any line may be sung once or twice or many times.)

I'm ready now, etc.
I'm singing now.
See my new shoes.
My new brown shoes.
I have a blue sweater.

I have red pants.
See Dicky's flower.
I have one too.
A silver bell.
Let's hear it ring.

The sun is shining.
The grass is wet.
I heard a robin.
The birds are singing.
I'm singing too.

(Perhaps someone starts turning around or running or jumping)

I'm turning round, etc.
Around and around.
Now turning the other way.
Around and around.
Jumping up and down now.

Running around now.
Sit down awhile.
And I lie down awhile.
I can close my eyes.
I can go to sleep.

Wake up now.
Open my eyes.
Stretch my toes.
Jumping up and down again.
Running around again.

How Old Are You?

I'LL BE SIXTEEN THIS SUNDAY

Moderately fast ♩=120

TEXAS

"How old are you, my pret-ty lit-tle miss? How old are you, my hon-ey?"

She an-swered me with a tee hee hee, "I'll be six-teen this Sun-day."

staccato throughout

REFRAIN (*may be omitted*)

The yad-dle lad-dle lad-dle um dai - sy, The yad-dle lad-dle lad-dle um,

Yad-dle lad-dle lad-dle um, Yad-dle lad-dle lad-dle um dai - sy.

2. Where are you going, my pretty little miss?
    Where are you going, my honey?
    She answered me with a tee hee hee,
    "I'm looking for my mummy."
    Refrain:

3. Where do you live, my pretty little miss? etc.
    "I live on the hill with mummy."
    Refrain:

4. What can you do, my pretty little miss? etc.
    "I can put on bread for mummy."
    Refrain:

*IMPROVISATION: Children can seldom wait beyond the second
line to tell how old they are, or where they live, or what they can do.*

How old are you, my pretty little miss (or good old man)?
How old are you, my honey?
"I'm four-and-a-half, I'm four-and-a-half,
I'm four-and-a-half this Sunday (or Monday or Tuesday, etc.)."

57

Jimmy Rose He Went to Town

Moderately fast ♩=100

Jim - my Rose he went to town, Jim - my Rose he went to town,

Jim - my Rose he went to town To 'com - mo - date the la - dies.

IMPROVISATION and RHYTHMIC PLAY: Jimmy Rose—or Raymond Horne or Paul Gregg or Timmy Wright—may be going away, or outdoors, or to rest, to lunch, to play, to school, to the store. Or he may be running around, or skipping, hopping, walking, jumping up and down, washing his hands, combing his hair, drinking his juice, "to commodate the ladies."

ACCOMPANIMENT: Speed and type of accompaniment may be adapted to the rhythmic play.

What Shall We Do When We All Go Out?

Moderately fast ♩ = 96

NORTH CAROLINA

What shall we do when we all go out, All go out, all go out,

What shall we do when we all go out, When we all go out to play?

IMPROVISATION and RHYTHMIC PLAY: Children have suggested many things, in song and motion.

1. We will ride our three-wheel bikes,
   Three-wheel bikes, three-wheel bikes,
   We will ride our three-wheel bikes
   When we all go out to play.

2. We will slide on the sliding board, etc.
3. We will see-saw up and down, etc.
4. We will pull our wagons 'round, etc.
5. We will climb the jungle-jim, etc.
6. We will dig in the sandpile, etc.
7. We will watch the beans grow, etc.
8. We will look for frogs' eggs, etc.
9. We will see the leaves fall, etc.

Goodbye, Julie

MISS JULIE ANN JOHNSON

Miss Ju - lie Ann John - son, o - ho!

Miss Ju - lie Ann John - son, o - ho!

Good - bye, _____ Ju - lie, o - ho!

Good - bye, _____ Ju - lie, o - ho!

2. Oh, where's my Julie? o-ho!
   Oh, where's my Julie? o-ho!
   She's gone to Dallas, o-ho!
   She's gone to Dallas, o-ho!

3. Going to catch that train, boys, o-ho!
   Going to catch that train, boys, o-ho!
   Going to find my Julie, o-ho!
   Going to find my Julie, o-ho!

4. Going to hug my Julie, o-ho!
   Going to hug my Julie, o-ho!
   Miss Julie Ann Johnson, o-ho!
   Miss Julie Ann Johnson, o-ho!

NAME PLAY: Each child likes to hear his name sung.

Goodbye. Robin, o-ho!
Goodbye. Eric, o-ho!
Goodbye. Connie, o-ho!
Goodbye. Karen, o-ho!

TONE PLAY:

Adult: Goodbye. Julie . . .
Child: . . . . o-ho!

Goodbye, Old Paint

Moderate ♩.= 60

WYOMING

REFRAIN

Good - bye, old Paint, I'm a - leav - ing Chey - enne,

Good - bye, old Paint, I'm a - leav - ing Chey - enne.

STANZA (may be played without singing, as piano interlude)

Old Paint's a good po - ny. He runs when he can, ___

D.C. al fine

Good morn - ing young la - dy, My po - ny won't stand. ___

62

REFRAIN:

Goodbye, old Paint,
I'm a-leaving Cheyenne,
Goodbye, old Paint,
I'm a-leaving Cheyenne.

2. I'm a-riding old Paint,
   I'm a-leading old Fan,
   Goodbye, little Annie,
   I'm off for Montan'.
   Refrain:

3. Oh, hitch up your horses,
   And feed them some hay,
   And seat yourself by me
   As long as you stay.
   Refrain:

4. My horses ain't hungry,
   They'll not eat your hay,
   My wagon is loaded
   And rolling away.
   Refrain:

It is said that this song was often used as a "Home, Sweet Home"
at the end of a cowboy dance—but as long as someone could remember
or improvise another stanza, the dance would go on.

63

Oh, Oh, the Sunshine

OH, OH, YOU CAN'T SHINE

Very Free

TEXAS

Oh, oh, the sun - shine!

Oh, oh, the sun - shine!

Oh, oh, the sun - shine!

Sal - ly's got a red dress, but - toned be - hind,

Sal - ly's got a red dress, but - toned be - hind.

IMPROVISATION:

1. Oh, oh, the sunshine!
   Oh, oh, the sunshine!
   Oh, oh, the sunshine!
   Susan's got blue overalls, buckled in front,
   Susan's got blue overalls, buckled in front.

or

2. Frankie's got brown shoes, laced on top, etc.
3. Jane's got a blue ribbon, tied in a bow, etc.
4. Anne has long hair, braided behind, etc.
5. Bruce has red socks, don't button at all, etc.

Sweet Water Rolling

SOUTH CAROLINA

Sweet wa-ter roll-ing, Sweet wa-ter roll,

Roll-ing from the foun-tain, Sweet wa-ter roll.

The Wind Blow East

NASSAU, BAHAMAS

Oh, the wind blow east,
The wind blow west,
The wind blow the *Setting Star*
Right down in town.
Refrain:

66

IMPROVISATION: The wind blows many things down into town —snowflakes, raindrops, autumn leaves, red leaves, yellow leaves, thunderclouds.

ACCOMPANIMENT: Clapping or drumming, or both, makes a natural accompaniment. In the Bahamas the song is accompanied with intricate and lively clapping, and the refrain is repeated as many as a dozen times.

Sunshine *and* Setting Star *are names of two ships which were blown "right down in town" during a hurricane in the Bahamas.*

Rain, Come Wet Me

Rain, come wet me. Sun, come dry me.

Keep a-way, pret-ty girls, Don't come a-nigh me.

It Rained a Mist

Moderate ♩.=60   VIRGINIA

It rained a mist, it rained a mist,

It rained all o-ver the town, town, town,

It rained all o-ver the town.   It

2. And all the boys went out to play
   A-tossing their ball around, round, round,
   A-tossing their ball around.

3. At first they tossed their ball too low,
   And then they tossed it too high, high, high,
   And then they tossed it too high.

4. They tossed it into a lady's garden
   Where roses and lilies lie, lie, lie,
   Where roses and lilies lie.

IMPROVISATION: Children sing about many objects it rains or snows over—the school big tree, the grass, the roof, even odd things like the piano, the floor, or "me, me, me."

Rain or Shine

DONEY GAL

TEXAS

A cowboy's life is a dreary thing,
For it's rope and brand and ride and sing,
Yes, day or night in the rain or hail,
He'll stay with his dogies out on the trail.
Refrain:

We whoop at the sun and yell through the hail,
But we drive the poor dogies down the trail,
And we'll laugh at the storms, the sleet and snow,
When we reach the little town of San Antonio.
Refrain:

69

One Cold and Frosty Morning

OLD JESSIE

Moderately fast ♩= 96

ALABAMA

One cold and frost-y morn-ing Just as the sun did rise,

The poss-um roared, the rac-coon howled, 'Cause he be-gan to freeze,

He drew him-self up in a knot, With his knees up to his chin,

And ev'-ry-thing had to clear the track When he stretched out a - gain.

REFRAIN

Old Jes-sie was a gen-tle-man A - mong the old-en times.

This is said to have been sung before the Civil War. One singer recalled that his father used it as a waking-up song for his children.

By'm Bye

STARS SHINING

TEXAS

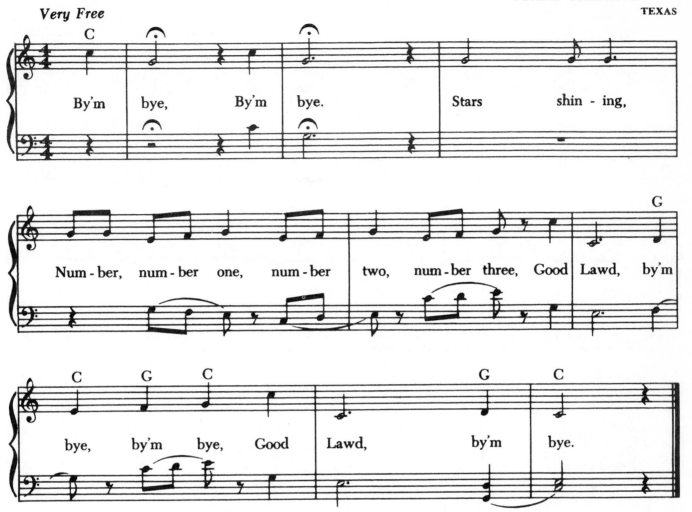

FINGER PLAY: *"Number, number one, number two, number three"—continuing on up to five or ten or more, if desired—may be used as a finger play. Many things may be counted aside from stars and fingers, such as buttons on clothing, or children, or stair steps, or foolish things like shoes untied.*

TONE PLAY: *Children echo* By'm Bye *without being asked, and like to join in on the numbering phrase, especially if it is extended through a growing series of numbers.*

Jim Along Josie

Moderately fast
OKLAHOMA

Hey jim a-long, jim a-long Jo-sie, Hey jim a-long, jim a-long Jo.

Hey jim a-long, jim a-long Jo-sie, Hey jim a-long, jim a-long Jo.

2. Walk jim along, jim along Josie,
    Walk jim along, jim along Jo. (*Repeat*)

3. Hop jim along, jim along Josie,
    Hop jim along, jim along Jo. (*Repeat*)

*IMPROVISATION and RHYTHMIC PLAY: Josie may have
thoughts or motions other than those in the traditional text given above.*

4. Run, jim along, jim along Josie, etc.
5. Jump, jim along, jim along Josie, etc.
6. Tiptoe along, jim along Josie, etc.
7. Crawl along, jim along, jim along Josie, etc.
8. Swing along, sing along, jim along Josie, etc.
9. Roll, jim along, jim along Josie, etc.

An invitation is sometimes appreciated:

Let's go walking, jim along Josie, etc.
Let's go running, jim along Josie, etc.
Let's sit down now, jim along Josie, etc.

*For rhythmic play the music should be repeated many times with-
out stopping. The words will probably be sung only once, or not at all.*

72

ACCOMPANIMENT: *Speed and type of accompaniment may be adapted to the various rhythmic activities. The sample variations which follow are suggestions only. Do not use them if you can make your own. In all of them the chordal basis is the same.*

The simple dance-song Jim Along Josie *is said to be based on an old minstrel song. It is widely known, especially as a game or play-party song. In some versions* Josie *appears to be the dance itself:*

Hold my mule while I dance Josie.

In a very old one, still sung, "Josie" is something to wear:

Who's been here since I been gone?
Pretty little girl with a josey on.

"Hey jim along" *is also sung* "Hey get along," "Hi come along,"
"Hey jam along," "Come-a-get along," "Come-a-high, jim along."

Moderately fast, heavy

5   Jump jim a - long,   jim a-long Jo - sie,   Jump jim a - long,   jim a - long Jo.

Moderately fast, very light

6   Tip - toe a - long,   jim a-long Jo - sie,   Tip - toe a - long,   jim a - long Jo.

Moderately slow, smooth

7   Crawl a-long jim   a-long,   jim a-long Jo-sie,   Crawl a-long jim a-long,   jim a-long Jo.

Moderate, smooth

8   Swing a-long,   sing a-long,   jim a-long Jo-sie,   Swing a-long,   sing a-long   jim a-long Jo.

A little fast, fluid.

9   Roll jim a-long, ___   jim a-long Jo - sie,   Roll jim a -long, ___   jim a-long Jo.

In skipping, time, bright

10 *mf*

Moderate, quiet

11 *p*

Let's sit down now, jim a-long Jo - sie, Let's sit down now, jim a-long Jo.

There Was a Man and He Was Mad

Moderately fast ♩ = 104

OHIO

There was a man and he was mad, And he jumped in-to the pud-ding bag.

2. The pudding bag it was so fine
   That he jumped into a bottle of wine.

3. The bottle of wine it was so clear
   That he jumped into a bottle of beer.

4. The bottle of beer it was so thick
   That he jumped into a walking stick.

5. The walking stick it was so narrow
   That he jumped into a wheel barrow.

6. The wheel barrow it did so crack
   That he jumped onto a horse's back.

7. The horse's back it did so bend
   That he jumped into a taching end.

8. The taching end it was so rotten
   That he jumped into a bag of cotton.

9. The bag of cotton it set on fire
   And blew him up to Jeremiah.

   (*spoken*)
   Pouf! Pouf! Pouf!

76

IMPROVISATION: Children as well as adults like to make new stanzas for this song. One mother and her child improvised a dozen couplets around the house. And a group of four-year-olds were so bowled over by the beer-bottle jump that they followed through, one morning, with hilarious adventures of their own—bubbles that wouldn't stop bubbling, a cork popping, an explosive flight skyward, and a long series of impractical encounters with airplanes.

RHYTHMIC PLAY: Various jumping plays are improvised during the singing of the song. Sometimes children like to take turns jumping over a stick held a few inches from the floor.

TONE PLAY:

Adult: And he jumped into the . . .
Child: . . . . pudding bag.

Riding in the Buggy, Miss Mary Jane

SOUTH CAROLINA

Moderately fast ♩= 104

Rid-ing in the bug-gy, Miss Ma-ry Jane, Miss Ma-ry Jane, Miss Ma-ry Jane,

Rid-ing in the bug-gy, Miss Ma-ry Jane, I'm a long ways from home.

REFRAIN

Who moan for me? Who moan for me?

Who moan for me, my darl-ing, Who moan for me?

2. Sally's got a house in Baltimore,
   In Baltimore, in Baltimore,
   Sally's got a house in Baltimore
   And it's full of chicken pie.
   Refrain:

3. I've got a girl in Baltimore,
   In Baltimore, in Baltimore,
   I've got a girl in Baltimore,
   And she's sixteen stories high.
   Refrain:

4. Fare you well, my little bitty Ann,
   My little bitty Ann, my little bitty Ann,
   Fare you well, my little bitty Ann,
   For I'm going away.
   Refrain:

*IMPROVISATION and RHYTHMIC PLAY: Miss Mary Jane may
ask to ride in a car, or on a trolley, an airplane, a camel, an elephant.
The accompaniment can be adapted accordingly. This is a favorite car
riding song while going to and from school.*

Billy Barlow

Moderately fast ♩. = 96

"Let's go hunt - ing," says Risk - y Rob,

"Let's go hunt - ing," says Rob - in to Bob,

"Let's go hunt - ing," says Dan' l to Joe,

"Let's _____ go hunt - ing," says Bil - ly Bar - low.

2. "What shall I hunt?" says Risky Rob,
   "What shall I hunt?" says Robin to Bob,
   "What shall I hunt?" says Dan'l to Joe,
   "Hunt for a rat," says Billy Barlow.

3. "How shall I get him?" says Risky Rob,
   "How shall I get him?" says Robin to Bob,
   "How shall I get him?" says Dan'l to Joe,
   "Go borrow a gun," says Billy Barlow.

4. "How shall I haul him?" etc. (3 times)
   "Go borrow a cart," said Billy Barlow.

5. "How shall we divide him?" etc. (4 times)

6. "I'll take shoulder," says Risky Rob,
   "I'll take side," says Robin to Bob,
   "I'll take ham," says Dan'l to Joe,
   "Tail bone mine," says Billy Barlow.

7. "How shall we cook him?" etc. (4 times)

8. "I'll broil shoulder," says Risky Rob,
   "I'll fry side," says Robin to Bob,
   "I'll boil ham," says Dan'l to Joe,
   "Tail bone raw," says Billy Barlow.

This is favorite skipping or skating music. Dramatic play may grow out of it with older children.

The Juniper Tree

ARKANSAS

Moderately fast ♩. = 96

O sis - ter Phoe - be, how mer - ry were we, The night we sat un - der the jun - i - per tree, The jun - i - per tree, Hi - o, hi - o, The jun - i - per tree, Hi - o.

2. Put this hat on your head to keep your head warm
   And one or two kisses will do you no harm,
   Will do you no harm, I know, I know,
   Will do you no harm, I know.

3. Go choose you a partner, go choose you a one,
   Go choose you the fairest that ever you can,
   Now rise you up, sister, and go, and go,
   Now rise you up, sister, and go.

RHYTHMIC PLAY and GAME: Small children like most to skip around freely to this music. Older children sometimes play the traditional singing game. During the first stanza they form a circle around a center child and skip or walk around him. During the second stanza someone from the circle puts a hat on his head. The center child then chooses another from the circle to take his place in the center, and the game is repeated. The third stanza may be omitted with small children.

Old Joe Clarke

ROUND AND ROUND

TENNESSEE

Round and round, old Joe Clarke, Round and round, I say,

Round and round, old Joe Clarke, I ain't got long to stay.

light staccato throughout

STANZA (*may be played without singing, as piano interlude*)

Old Joe Clarke he had a house, Six-teen sto-ries high,

Ev'-ry sto-ry in that house Was full of chick-en pie.

Old Joe Clarke is a well-known square-dance tune. All the traditional refrains lend themselves to free rhythmic play. This song has often drawn a group of children together when nothing else would.

OTHER REFRAINS:

Rock-a-rock, old Joe Clarke,
Rock-a-rock, I'm gone;
Rock-a-rock, old Joe Clarke,
And goodbye, Susan Brown.

Fly around, old Joe Clarke,
Fly around, I'm gone;
Fly around, old Joe Clarke,
With the golden slippers on.

Row around, old Joe Clarke,
Sail away and gone;
Row around, old Joe Clarke,
With golden slippers on.

Roll, roll, old Joe Clarke,
Roll, roll, I say;
Roll, roll, old Joe Clarke,
You'd better be gettin' away.

OTHER STANZAS:

Old Joe Clarke he had a dog
As blind as he could be;
Chased a redbug 'round a stump
And a coon up a hollow tree.

I went down to old Joe's house,
Never been there before,
He slept on the feather bed
And I slept on the floor.

If you see that girl of mine,
Tell her if you can,
Before she goes to make up bread
To wash those dirty hands.

When I was a little boy
I used to play in ashes
Now I am a great big boy
Wearing Dad's mustaches.

IMPROVISATION and RHYTHMIC PLAY: Children have always been fond of turning around and around until they are dizzy, then falling down.

REFRAIN:

Round and round, old Joe Clarke,
Round and round, I say,
Round and round, old Joe Clarke,
I ain't got long to stay.

STANZA:

Round and round and round, I turn,
Round and round, I say,
Round and round and round I turn
And . . .

    (spoken)
        NOW FALL DOWN!
And . . .

        NOW UP AGAIN!
And . . .

    REFRAIN (singing again):

        Round and round, old Joe Clarke,
        Round the other way, etc.

Clap Your Hands

IMPROVISATION and RHYTHMIC PLAY: *This entire song has been adapted from the dance song Old Joe Clarke (page 84). Many of the motions came first from the children: in the middle of a song someone would start tapping toes or stamping feet.*

2. Stamp, stamp, stamp your feet,
    Stamp your feet together,
    Stamp, stamp, stamp your feet,
    Stamp your feet together.

3. Tap, tap, tap your toes, etc.
4. Nod, nod, nod your head, etc.
5. Shake, shake, shake your hands, etc.
6. Stretch, stretch, stretch up high, etc.
7. Wheels, wheels going round, etc.
8. Dig, dig, dig the ground, etc.
9. See, see, see the moon, etc.
10. Sing, sing, sing a song, etc.

Down by the Greenwood Sidey-o

A ball may be rolled back and forth to the rhythm of singing. The song should be sung with strong accent, but smoothly. "Babes" may be changed to "children."

Roll That Brown Jug Down to Town

ILLINOIS

2. Big 'tatoes grow in sandy land,
   Big 'tatoes grow in sandy land,
   Big 'tatoes grow in sandy land,
   Way down in Alabam'.

3. Sift that meal and save the bran, etc.

IMPROVISATION and RHYTHMIC PLAY: A ball-rolling game is fun, the children sitting either in a line or a semicircle, and the adult rolling the ball to each in turn.

Roll that red ball down to town,
Roll that red ball down to town,
Roll that red ball down to town,
So early in the morning.

The song can also roll on through endless series of variations. Chuck kept it going one day through a dozen or more.

1. Ride that big bike down to town.
2. Jump that little Jack down to town.

3. Walk that little dog home again.
4. Roll your little self down to school,
   and so on.

And when one of the children didn't want to go to bed, a never-stopping song about each process made her laugh out loud. It began downstairs:

Roll that little girl up the steps,

and continued through each piece of clothing
Pull that blue shirt over your head,

and ended with bed
Roll that little girl into bed.

As I Walked Out One Holiday

A LITTLE BOY THREW HIS BALL SO HIGH

VIRGINIA

Moderate ♩. = 60

1. As I walked out one hol - i - day, The flakes of snow did fall,
2. A lit-tle boy threw his ball so high, He threw his ball so low,

And all the chil - dren in the school Were out a - play - ing ball.
He threw it in a dusk - y gar-den A - mong the blades of snow.

3. Out came the neighbor's youngest daughter
   All dressed in fairy green.
   "Come in, come in, my lad," she said,
   "You may have your ball again."

She'll Be Coming Round the Mountain When She Comes

2. She'll be driving six white horses when she comes,
   She'll be driving six white horses when she comes,
   She'll be driving six white horses,
   She'll be driving six white horses,
   She'll be driving six white horses when she comes.

3. Oh, we'll all go out to meet her when she comes, etc.

4. Oh, we'll all have chicken and dumplin's when she comes, etc.

Juba

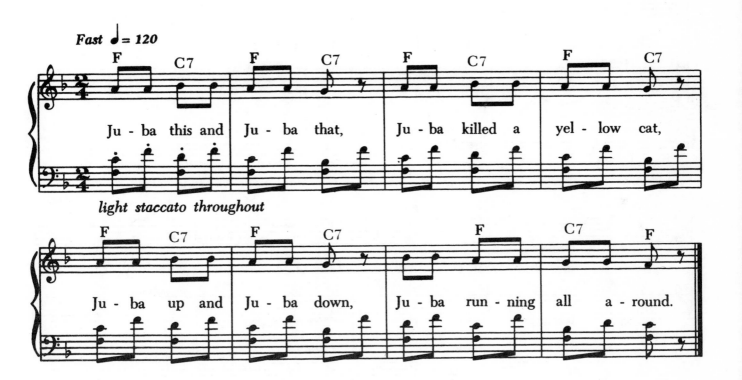

Juba may have, or see, or find, or chase the yellow cat, and jump, hop, dance, clap hands, pat knees.

Juba is an old "patting" song and dance which is still known and danced by all ages. It is often half sung, half spoken, to the accompaniment of fast clapping and patting of the knees and, occasionally, intricate footwork.

Run, Chillen, Run

Fast ♩ = 120
REFRAIN

Run, chil-len, run, the pat-ter-roll-er catch you, Run, chil-len, run, it's al-most day.

light staccato throughout

Run, chil-len, run, the pat-ter-roll-er catch you, Run, chil-len, run, it's al-most day.

Fine

STANZA (*if too high for easy singing, the words can be spoken or the tune whistled, while playing.*)

That child ran, and that child flew, That child lost his Sun-day shoe.

D.C. al fine

REFRAIN:

Run, chillen, run, the patterroller catch you,
Run, chillen, run, it's almost day.
Run, chillen, run, the patterroller catch you,
Run, chillen, run, it's almost day.

2. Jumped the fence and ran through the pasture,
    First ran slow and then he ran faster.
    Refrain:

3. Let me tell you what I'll do,
    I'm going to find me a Sunday shoe.
    Refrain:

4. Let me tell you where I'll be,
    I'm going to hide behind that tree.
    Refrain:

A patterroller was a patrolman whose job it was, in pre-Civil-War days, to patrol plantation borders. In some localities the workers were allowed to visit neighboring plantations but had to be back before daybreak.

All Around the Kitchen
COCKY DOODLE DOODLE DOO

RHYTHMIC PLAY: *Children react to this perky song with various sorts of body play, especially if the music is repeated many times without stopping. In one room there were four tall posts. Someone started going around one of them—and soon each post was the center of an orbit.*

GAME: *Older children may like to play the game as it was played in Alabama. The children form a circle around a center child and "march or skip" while singing. Then they stand still while the singer in the center "makes a motion," as her ingenuity dictates. She may kneel, prance, bow, dance a jig, or otherwise cavort. Sometimes the player chooses the motion and the others must follow her example, must "do it like this."*

I'm Going to Join the Army

Moderately fast ♩ = 104

KENTUCKY

vamp ad lib

I'm going to join the ar-my, I'm going to vol-un-teer,

I'm going to be a sol-dier Be-fore an-o-ther year.

2. May I go with you, Johnny?
   I'll travel by your side,
   And when the battle's over
   You'll make me your bride.

3. Yes, come go with me, Sally,
   And travel by my side,
   And when the battle's over
   I'll make you my bride.

Scraping Up Sand in the Bottom of the Sea

SHILOH

Fast ♩ = 126

MISSOURI

vamp ad lib

Scrap-ing up sand in the bot-tom of the sea, Shi-loh, Shi-loh,

Scrap-ing up sand in the bot-tom of the sea, Shi-loh, Li-za Jane.

REFRAIN

Oh, how I love her, Oh, Li-za Jane,

Oh, how I love her, Good-bye, Li-za Jane.

Ending

2. Black those shoes and make them shine,
   Shiloh, shiloh,
   Black those shoes and make them shine,
   Shiloh, Liza Jane.
   Refrain:

3. A hump-back mule I'm bound to ride, etc.
   Refrain:

4. Hopped up a chicken and he flew upstairs, etc.
   Refrain:

RHYTHMIC PLAY and FINGER PLAY: Dredging machines—and whales—scoop up sand from the bottom of the sea. Steam shovels scoop it up from the vacant lot down the street where a new house is being built. Small garden shovels scoop it up to make the ground ready for seeds. Fingers scoop up sand too, scrape it and sift it through endless repetitions of the first two lines of this song.

Old Mister Rabbit

Moderately fast ♩ = 100

Old Mis-ter Rab - bit, You've got a might-y hab - it Of

jump-ing in the gar - den And eat-ing all my cab - bage.

IMPROVISATION and RHYTHMIC PLAY: *Old Mister Rabbit may eat all sorts of vegetables. And of course he will jump all over the garden.*

TONE PLAY:

Adult: And eating all my . . .
Child: . . . . cabbage.

ACCOMPANIMENT: *The chords may be arpeggiated if desired:*

Old Molly Hare

Very fast ♩ = 120

Old Mol - ly Hare, _____ What you do - ing there? ___

Run - ning through the cot - ton patch As fast as I can tear.

2. Old Molly Hare,
What you doing there?
Sitting in my fireplace
A-smoking my cigar.

3. Old Molly Hare,
What you doing there?
Sitting on a haystack
A-shooting at a bear.

4. Old Molly Hare,
What you doing there?
Sitting on a butter-plate
A-picking out a hair.

5. Old Molly Hare,
Your tail's too short,
Yes, doggone it,
I can tuck it out of sight.

6. Dogs say "boo"
And they bark too,
I haven't got the time
For to talk to you.

7. Riding of a goat
And leading of a sheep
I won't be back
Till the middle of the week.

99

Oh, John the Rabbit

Moderately fast ♩= 88

MISSISSIPPI

Oh, John the Rab-bit, Yes ma'am,

Got a might-y hab-it, Yes ma'am,

Jum-ping in my gar-den, Yes ma'am,

Cut-ting down my cab-bage, Yes ma'am,

My sweet po-ta-toes, Yes ma'am,

My fresh to-ma-toes, Yes ma'am,

And if I live, — Yes ma'am, To see next fall, — Yes ma'am,

I ain't gon-na have, Yes ma'am, No cot-ton at all, Yes ma'am.

IMPROVISATION: The list of vegetables may be extended. Or other habits may be sung about, with details changing from day to day. John does many things in the morning. The music for lines 3 to 7 below may be repeated with as many new words as the children can think of, before finishing the song.

Oh, John the Rabbit, Yes ma'am,
Got a mighty habit, Yes ma'am,
Jumping up in the morning, Yes ma'am,

Putting on his clothes, Yes ma'am,
His socks and shoes, Yes ma'am,
His shirt and pants, Yes ma'am,

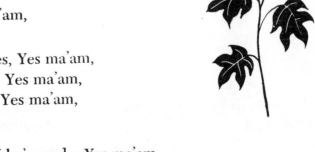

And if he's ready, Yes ma'am,
By half-past eight, Yes ma'am,
He can go to school, Yes ma'am,
And he won't be late, Yes ma'am.

The Little Pig

Moderately fast ♩ = 104

There was an old wom-an and she had a lit-tle pig, ___ Oink, oink, oink,

There was an old wom-an and she had a lit-tle pig,

It did-n't cost much and was-n't ver-y big, ___ Oink, oink, oink.

2. That little pig did a heap of harm,
      Oink, oink, oink,
   That little pig did a heap of harm
   A-rooting 'round the old man's farm,
      Oink, oink, oink.

3. The little pig died for want of breath, etc.
   Now wasn't that an awful death! etc.

4. The little old woman, she sobbed and she sighed, etc.
   Then she lay right down and died, etc.

5. The old man died for want of grief, etc.
   Wasn't that a great relief! etc.

6. There they lay all one two three, etc.
   The man and the woman and the little piggee, etc.

7. There they lay all on the shelf, etc.
   If you want any more you can sing it yourself, etc.

RHYTHMIC and DRAMATIC PLAY: The first two stanzas lend themselves to free rhythmic play. The singing of the entire song may call forth simple dramatic play. Or out of some child's action or word may grow—sometimes expanding or changing from day to day—an unexpected play sequence. This happened one morning when a "pig" lay down and "went to sleep."

2. Those little pigs curled up in a heap,
        Oink, oink, oink,
   Those little pigs curled up in a heap,
   They shut their eyes and went to sleep,
        Oink, oink, oink.

3. They slept and slept and slept and slept,
        Sh—sh—sh—
   They slept and slept and slept and slept
   And slept and slept and slept and slept—
        Sh—sh—sh—

4. The farmer woke them one by one
        Oink, oink, oink,
   The farmer woke them one by one
   And then they rolled out in the sun
        Oink, oink, oink.

5. They rolled and rolled and rolled and rolled, etc.
        The music of this stanza may be repeated ad lib—and then:

6. Those little pigs rolled back in their pen
        Oink, oink, oink,
   Those little pigs rolled back in their pen
   And then they went to sleep again
        Oink, oink, oink.

Bought Me a Cat

3. Bought me a duck, the duck pleased me, Fed my duck un-der yon-ders tree.

Duck went slish - y slosh-y.
Hen went chip - sy chop-sy, Cat went fid-dle-i-fee, fid-dle-i-fee.

4. Bought me a goose, the goose pleased me, Fed my goose un-der yon-ders tree.

Goose went qua,
Duck went slish-y slosh-y.
Hen went chip-sy chop-sy, Cat went fid-dle-i-fee, fid-dle-i-fee.

105

5. Bought me a dog, the dog pleased me, Fed my dog un-der yon-ders tree.

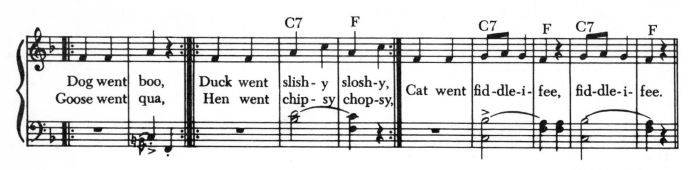

Dog went boo,
Goose went qua,
Duck went slish-y slosh-y,
Hen went chip-sy chop-sy,
Cat went fid-dle-i- fee, fid-dle-i- fee.

6. Bought me a sheep, the sheep pleased me, Fed my sheep un-der yon-ders tree.

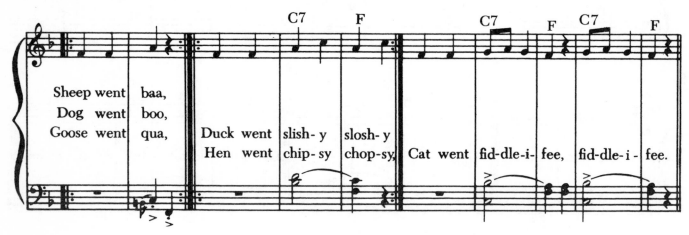

Sheep went baa,
Dog went boo,
Goose went qua,
Duck went slish-y slosh-y
Hen went chip-sy chop-sy, Cat went fid-dle-i- fee, fid-dle-i - fee.

7. Bought me a cow, the cow pleased me, Fed my cow un-der yon-ders tree,

Cow went moo,
Sheep went baa,
Dog went boo,
Goose went qua,
Duck went slish-y slosh-y
Hen went chip-sy chop-sy, Cat went fid-dle-i- fee, fid-dle-i- fee.

8. Bought me a horse, the horse pleased me, Fed my horse un-der yon-ders tree,

Horse went neigh,
Cow went moo,
Sheep went baa,
Dog went boo,
Goose went qua,
Duck went slish-y slosh-y,
Hen went chip-sy chop-sy, Cat went fid-dle-i- fee, fid-dle-i- fee.

9. Bought me a ba-by, the ba-by pleased me, Fed my ba-by un-der yon-ders tree,

Ba-by went mam-my, mam-my,
Horse went neigh,
Cow went moo,
Sheep went baa,
Dog went boo,
Goose went qua,
Duck went slish-y, slosh-y,
Hen went chip-sy chop-sy Cat *etc*

10. Bought me a wo-man, the wo-man pleased me, Fed my wo-man un-der yon-ders tree,

Wo-man went Hon-ey, Hon-ey,
Ba-by went mam-my, mam-my,
Horse went neigh,
Cow went moo,
Sheep went baa,
Dog went boo,
Goose went qua,
Duck went slish-y slosh-y,
Hen went chip-sy chop-sy Cat *etc*

108

Hop, Old Squirrel

Moderately fast ♩ = 112

VIRGINIA

Hop, old squirrel, ei-dle-dum, ei-dle-dum, Hop old squirrel, ei-dle-dum dum,

Hop, old squirrel, ei-dle-dum, ei-dle-dum, Hop, old squirrel, ei-dle-dum dee.

The following traditional words can form a basis of selection for various games. One group of children, many years ago in Virginia, were seen running from tree to tree singing some of them.

1. Hide, old squirrel, eidledum, eidledum, etc.
2. Hunt for the squirrel, etc.
3. Peep, little squirrel, etc.
4. Find the old squirrel, etc.
5. Run, old squirrel, etc.
6. Chase the old squirrel, etc.
7. Catch the old squirrel, etc.
8. Bring in the old squirrel, etc.

RHYTHMIC PLAY:

1. Hop, little bird, eidledum, eidledum, etc.
2. Hop (or leap) old frog, etc.
3. Hop on one foot, etc.

My Horses Ain't Hungry

INTRODUCTION (*may be omitted*)

(*The horses are in the barn, eating hay*)

etc. ad lib

Moderately fast ♩. = 60

My hors - es ain't hun - gry, They won't eat your hay,

So I'll get on my po - ny, I'm go - ing a - way.

INTERLUDE (*faster, for rhythmic play*)

Repeat ad lib

2. I know you're my Polly,
   I'm not going to stay,
   So come with me, darling,
   We'll feed on our way.

3. With all our belongings
   We'll ride till we come
   To a lonely little cabin,
   We'll call it our home.

RHYTHMIC and DRAMATIC PLAY: Various rhythmic, dramatic, and finger plays grow out of singing this much-loved song. One of the simplest involves the first stanza only: choosing a barn, quiet waiting for the song to begin, extended galloping when the music goes faster—and then, usually, returning to the barn for repetition of the game. Four- and five-year-olds sometimes like to go on to the second and third stanza, discover a cabin, and set up housekeeping.

IMPROVISATION: An adaptation based on Laura Pendleton MacCarteney's Little Gray Ponies *is liked by very small children:*

1. Little horses, little horses,
   Come out of your barn,
   The door is wide open,
   The sunshine is warm.

Interlude (same music played faster ad lib, for galloping)—then:

2. Little horses, little horses,
   Come back to your barn,
   The door is wide open,
   Your blankets are warm.

Did You Go to the Barney?

ARKANSAS

Free

Did you go to the barn-ey? Yes ma'am.

Did you see my mu - lie? Yes ma'am.

Did you ride my mu - lie? Yes ma'am.

And how did he ride? *smooth*

REFRAIN (may be played over and over for rhythmic play)

He rocked just like a cra-dle, He rocked just like a cra-dle.

Ending

2. Did you go to the barney? Yes ma'am.
Did you see my mulie? Yes ma'am.
Did you feed my mulie? Yes ma'am.
And what did you feed him?
I fed him corn and fodder,
I fed him corn and fodder.

3. Did you go to the millie? Yes ma'am.
Did you get any flour? Yes ma'am.
Did you bake any cakes? Yes ma'am.
And why did you bake them?
Oh, I'll marry next Thursday morning,
Oh, I'll marry next Thursday morning.

IMPROVISATION and RHYTHMIC PLAY: Children ask to ride or feed other animals and things—ponies, elephants, bicycles, ice skates. They want to sing about going to the firehouse, to the store, to the zoo. The questions and answers make new stanzas.

Did you go to the firehouse? Yes ma'am.
Did you see my fire engine? Yes ma'am.
Did you ride my fire engine? Yes ma'am.
And how did it ride?

The rest of the music may be played over and over without singing, for free rhythmic play.

Did you go to the zoo? Yes ma'am.
Did you see my tiger? Yes ma'am.
Did you feed my tiger? No ma'am.
And why didn't you feed him?
He slept up on the shelf,
He slept up on the shelf.

TONE PLAY:

Adult: Did you go to the barney? . . .
Child: . . . . Yes ma'am.

Sometimes "No ma'am" is answered with a glint in the eye, and a whole group becomes imbued with the fun of saying it.

Have a Little Dog

TOLL-A-WINKER

Fast ♩=100

TEXAS

Have a lit-tle dog and his name is Don (*whistle*_____)

Have a lit-tle dog and his name is Don,

His legs go to feet and his bod-y goes to tongue,

Toll- a - wink- er, toll- a -wink- er, tum tol - ly - aye.

114

2. Have a little box about three feet square (*whistle*)
   Have a little box about three feet square,
   When I go to travel I put him in there,
   Toll-a-winker, toll-a-winker, tum tolly-aye.

3. When I go to travel I travel like an ox, (*whistle*) (*2 times*)
   And in my vest pocket I carry that box, etc.

4. Had a little hen and her color was fair, (*whistle*) (*2 times*)
   Sat her on a bomb and she hatched me a hare, etc.

5. The hare turned a horse about six feet high, (*whistle*) (*2 times*)
   If you want to beat this you'll have to tell a lie, etc.

OTHER STANZAS:

1. I had a little mule and his name was Jack.
   I rode him on his tail to save his back.

2. I had a little mule and his name was Jay,
   I pulled his tail to hear him bray.

3. I had a little mule who was quite slick,
   I pulled his tail to see him kick.

4. This little mule he kicked so high,
   I thought that I had touched the sky.

5. I had a little mule he was made of hay,
   First big wind come along and blowed him away.

Frog Went A-Courtin'

Moderately fast ♩ = 112

VIRGINIA

Frog went a-court-in' and he did ride, ___ M - hm,

Frog went a-court-in' and he did ride, ___ M - hm,

Frog went a-court-in' and he did ride, ___

Sword and pis-tol by his side, ___ M - hm.

2. Rode right up to Miss Mouse's door, M-hm,
   Rode right up to Miss Mouse's door, M-hm,
   Rode right up to Miss Mouse's door,
   Gave three raps and a very loud roar, M-hm.

3. Said he, "Miss Mouse, are you within?" M-hm, etc.
   "Yes, kind sir, I sit and spin, M-hm."

4. He took Miss Mousie on his knee,
   Said, "Miss Mouse, will you marry me?"

5. "Without my Uncle Rat's consent,
   I wouldn't marry the President."

6. Uncle Rat he laughed and shook his fat sides,
   To think his niece would be a bride.

7. Uncle Rat went a-running down to town
   To buy his niece a wedding gown.

8. "Where shall the wedding supper be?"
   "Way down yonder in the hollow tree."

9. "What shall the wedding supper be?"
   "A fried mosquito and a black-eyed pea."

10. First to come in was a flying moth,
    She laid out the table cloth.

11. Next to come in a Juney bug,
    Carrying a water jug.

12. Next to come in was a bumberly bee,
    Set his fiddle on his knee.

13. Next to come in was a broken-backed flea,
    Danced a jig with the bumberly bee.

14. Next to come in was Missus Cow,
    Tried to dance but didn't know how.

15. Next to come in was a little black tick,
    Ate so much it made him sick.

16. Next to come in was Doctor Fly,
    Said Mister Tick would surely die.

17. Next to come in was a big black snake,
    Ate up all the wedding cake.

18. Next to come in was an old gray cat,
    She swallowed the mouse and ate up the rat.

19. Mister Frog went a-hopping over the brook,
    A lily-white duck came and swallowed him up.

20. Little piece of cornbread lying on the shelf,
    If you want any more you can sing it yourself.

Little Bird, Little Bird

Very fast ♩= 112

SOUTH CAROLINA

Lit-tle bird, lit-tle bird, go through my win-dow,

Lit-tle bird, lit-tle bird, go through my win-dow,

Lit-tle bird, lit-tle bird, go through my win-dow, And buy mo-lass-es can-dy.

REFRAIN

Go through my win-dow, my su-gar lump, Go through my win-dow, my su-gar lump,

And buy mo-lass-es can-dy.

Blue bird, blue bird,
Fly through my window,
Blue bird, blue bird,
Fly through my window,
Blue bird, blue bird,
Fly through my window,
And buy molasses candy.

REFRAIN:

Fly through my window,
My little bird,
Fly through my window,
My little bird,
And buy molasses candy.

RHYTHMIC PLAY: This song lends itself to free rhythmic play as well as to simple game playing.

TWO GAMES:

Two children join hands and hold arms high to form an arch. The others pass beneath, one by one.

All the children except one form a circle with hands joined and arms arched to form windows. The remaining child goes in and out the windows.

Free Little Bird

2. Oh, who will shoe your little foot,
   And who will glove your little hand,
   And who will kiss your sweet rosy cheeks
   When I'm gone to that far distant land?

3. Oh, it's mama will shoe my little foot,
   And it's papa will glove my little hand,
   And it's you shall kiss my sweet rosy cheeks
   When you come from that far distant land.

4. Take me home, little birdie, take me home,
   Take me home by the light of the moon,
   With the moon a-shining bright and the stars a-giving light
   Take me home to my mama, take me home.

Poor Old Crow

THE THREE RAVENS

VIRGINIA

Ducks in the Millpond

Fast ♩=112

VIRGINIA

Ducks in the mill - pond, a - geese in the clo - ver, a -

Fell in the mill - pond, a - wet all o - ver.

REFRAIN

Lawd, Lawd, _____ gon - na get on a rink - tum,

Lawd, Lawd, _____ gon - na get on a rink - tum.

2. Ducks in the millpond, a-geese in the clover,
   Jumped in the bed, and the bed turned over.

   REFRAIN:

   Lawd, Lawd, gonna get on a rinktum,
   Lawd, Lawd, gonna get on a rinktum.

3. Monkey in the barnyard, a-monkey in the stable,
   Monkey get your hair cut as soon as you're able.
   Refrain:

4. Had a little pony, his name was Jack,
   I put him in the stable and he jumped through a crack.
   Refrain:

5. Ducks in the millpond, a-geese in the ocean,
   A-hug them pretty girls if I take a notion.
   Refrain:

Jim Crack Corn

BIG OLD OWL

VIRGINIA

Big old owl with eyes so bright, On man-y a dark and star-ry night,

I've of-ten heard my true love say, "Sing all night and sleep all day."

REFRAIN

Jim ___ crack corn, I don't care, Jim ___ crack corn, I don't care,

Jim ___ crack corn, I don't care, Old Mas-ter's gone a-way.

2. Said the blackbird to the crow:
    Down to the cornfield let us go;
    Pulling up corn has been our trade,
    Ever since Adam and Eve was made.
    Refrain:

3. Said the sheldrake to the crane:
    When do you think we'll have some rain?
    The farm's so muddy and the brook so dry,
    If it wasn't for the tadpoles, we'd all die.
    Refrain:

4. When I was a boy I used to wait
    On Master's table and pass the plate,
    Hand round the bottle when he got dry,
    And brush away the blue-tail fly.
    Refrain:

This version of the well-known minstrel song Jim Crack Corn *was notated from a phonograph recording of the singing of an old man, who states on the record that he in turn learned it from an aged banjo picker when he himself was a small boy.*

Eency Weency Spider

NORTH CAROLINA

Moderately fast ♩. = 104

Een - cy ween - cy spi - der went up the wa - ter spout,

Down came the rain_____ and washed the spi - der out,

Out came the sun_____ and dried up all the rain,

Now een - cy ween - cy spi - der went up the spout a - gain.

This is a favorite finger play.

126

Dog Tick

LOUISIANA

Moderately fast ♩ = 120

Dog tick, dog tick, dog tick, 'bac - co worm,

Why can't a dog tick dance ___ like a 'bac - co worm?

Dog tick, dog tick, dog tick, 'bac - co worm,

Why can't a dog tick dance ___ like a 'bac - co worm?

Who Built the Ark? Noah, Noah

Moderately fast ♩=76
REFRAIN

Who built the ark? No-ah, No-ah,

Who built the ark? Bro-ther No-ah built the ark.

STANZAS (*sing 1, 2, 3, 4, then return to refrain*)

1. Now didn't old No - ah build the ark?
2. built it long, both wide and tall,
3. found him an axe, and ham - mer too, Be -
4. ev' - ry time that ham - mer ring,

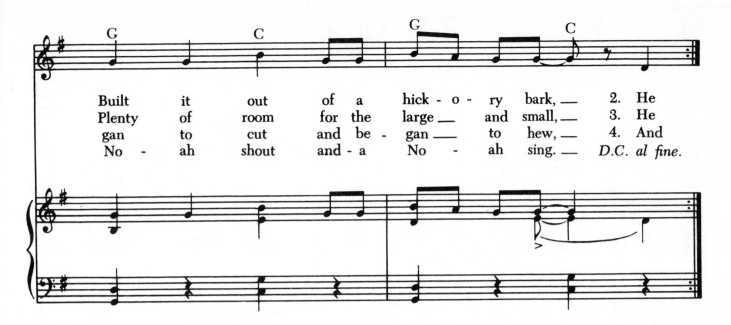

Built it out of a hick - o - ry bark, — 2. He
Plenty of room for the large __ and small, __ 3. He
gan to cut and be - gan __ to hew, — 4. And
No - ah shout and - a No - ah sing. — *D.C. al fine.*

5. Now in come the animals two by two,
   Hippopotamus and kangaroo,

6. Now in come the animals three by three,
   Two big cats and a bumble bee,

7. Now in come the animals four by four,
   Two through the window and two through the door,

8. Now in come the animals five by five,
   Four little sparrows and the redbird's wife,

9. Now in come the animals six by six,
   Elephant laughed at the monkey's tricks,

10. Now in come the animals seven by seven,
    Four from home and the rest from heaven,

11. Now in come the animals eight by eight,
    Some were on time and the others were late,

12. Now in come the animals nine by nine,
    Some was a-shouting and some was a-crying,

13. Now in come the animals ten by ten,
    Five black roosters and five black hens,

14. Now Noah says, go shut that door,
    The rain's started dropping and we can't take more.

Return to Refrain

129

Mary Wore Her Red Dress

Moderately fast ♩ = 112

Ma - ry wore her red dress, Red dress, red dress,

Ma - ry wore her red dress All day long.

2. Mary wore her red hat,
   Red hat, red hat,
   Mary wore her red hat
   All day long.

3. Mary wore her red shoes, etc.
4. Mary wore her red gloves, etc.
5. Mary made a red cake, etc.
6. Where'd you get your shoes from, etc.
7. Got them from the dry goods, etc.
8. Where'd you get your butter from, etc.
9. Got it from the grocery, etc.
10. Mary was a red bird, etc.

130

IMPROVISATION and NAME PLAY: When you ask children what piece of clothing they want to sing about, you get a wide assortment of answers. Even the most cumbersome can be fitted to the tune by the traditional practice of inserting extra beats for the extra syllables (see page 28).

Sing about my new dirty brown shoes.
Sing about my red-dress-with-green-and-yellow-flowers.
Sing about my very old overalls.
Sing about my knees.
Sing about my head.
Sing about my red-and-blue-and-black-and-white-striped socks.
Sing about the yellow-sweater-my-mommy-brought-me-from-
   New-York.

Out of daily incidents or a word or a motion arise other things to sing about. Brennan appears with a red ball or a fresh bandage on her finger, Philip has been dyeing Easter eggs yellow, Chris sees a caterpillar and starts crawling, Louis looks out the window and sees snow falling.

COLOR GAME: A color-guessing game is fun. It helps children to notice and to listen.

Who wore a pink dress,
Pink dress, pink dress,
Who wore a pink dress
All day long?

Elsa wore a pink dress,
Pink dress, pink dress,
Nancy wore a pink dress
All day long.

Pretty Little Girl with the Red Dress On

Moderately fast ♩ = 120

Poor old How - ard's dead and gone, Left me here to sing this song,
Who's been here since I been gone? Pretty little girl with the red dress on,

REFRAIN

Pret-ty lit-tle girl with the red dress on,

Pret-ty lit-tle girl with the red dress on,

Pret-ty lit-tle girl with the red dress on, who knows,

Pret-ty lit-tle girl with the red dress on.

This Lady She Wears a Dark Green Shawl

Moderately fast ♩ = 80

GEORGIA

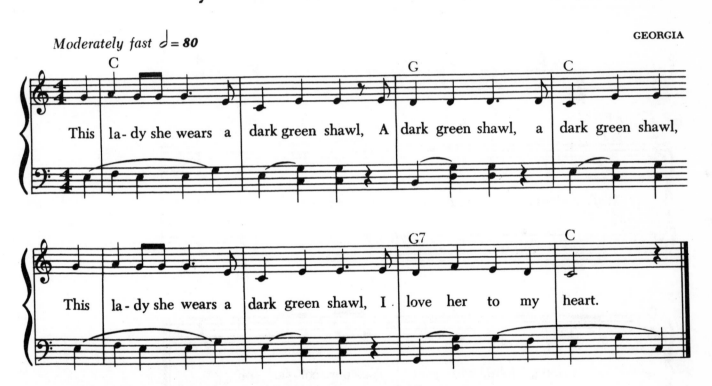

This la-dy she wears a dark green shawl, A dark green shawl, a dark green shawl,

This la-dy she wears a dark green shawl, I love her to my heart.

This too is a favorite name, color and clothing song. The remaining traditional stanzas are really singing-game directions:

2. Now choose you a partner, honey my love,
   Honey my love, honey my love,
   Now choose you a partner, honey my love,
   I love you to my heart.

3. Now dance with your partner, honey my love, etc.

4. Farewell to your partner, honey my love, etc.

133

Walk Along, John

Moderately fast ♩ = 88

OKLAHOMA

Come on, boys, and hush your talk - ing,

All join hands and let's go walk - ing.

REFRAIN

Walk a - long, John, with your pa - per col - lar on,

Walk a - long, John, with your pa - per col - lar on.

134

*IMPROVISATION and RHYTHMIC PLAY: One by one, a group
of walkers may be drawn together.*

Come on, Bill, and hush your talking,
Let's join hands and go a-walking,
Walk along, Bill, with your blue pants on,
Walk along, Bill, with your blue pants on.

*If there are many children, the refrain may be repeated over and
over with only an occasional return to the beginning.*

Walk (or come) along, Judy, with one shoe on,
Walk along, Janet, with your hair falling down,
Walk along, Mike, with your dad's old hat,
                    and so on.

*In one section of the country this song is said to have been sung as
a corn shucking song, with the following refrain:*

Shock along, John, shock along,
Shock along, John, shock along.

Do, Do, Pity My Case

Moderately fast ♩ = 88   LOUISIANA

Do, do, pi- ty my case, In some la - dy's gar - den,

My clothes to wash when I get home, In some la - dy's gar - den.

IMPROVISATION and DRAMATIC PLAY: Children have car-
ried through in free rhythmic play the activities of an entire afternoon.
The accompaniment may be adapted accordingly. Many of the activities—such as sewing or washing hands—become finger plays. Such
stanzas as the following have been improvised; they change from day
to day.

1. Do, do, pity my case,
   In some lady's garden,
   My hands to wash when I get home,
   In some lady's garden.

2. My cat to feed when I get home, etc.

3. To set the table when I get home, etc.

4. To have some cake when I get home, etc.

5. My nap to take when I get home, etc.

6. To see my dad when I get home, etc.

7. To dig my garden when I get home, etc.

8. To watch the robins when I get home, etc.

Hanging Out the Linen Clothes

2. 'Twas on a Tuesday morning, the first I saw my darling
   A-hanging out the linen clothes, a-hanging out the linen clothes

3. 'Twas on a Wednesday morning, the first I saw my darling
   A-taking in the linen clothes, a-taking in the linen clothes.

4. 'Twas on a Thursday morning, the first I saw my darling
   A-ironing of the linen clothes, a-ironing of the linen clothes.

5. 'Twas on a Friday morning, the first I saw my darling
   A-mending of the linen clothes, a-mending of the linen clothes.

6. 'Twas on a Saturday morning, the first I saw my darling
   A-folding of the linen clothes, a-folding of the linen clothes.

7. 'Twas on a Sunday morning, the first I saw my darling
   A-wearing of the linen clothes, a-wearing of the linen clothes.

Sometimes the last line of each stanza is sung over and over until the clothes are thoroughly "washed" or "ironed" or "mended."

Lula Gal

TIE MY SHOE

Moderately fast, accented ♩ = 96

Lu - la gal, Lu - la gal, Lu - la gal, Lu - la gal,

Tie my shoe, boy, tie my shoe, Tie my shoe, boy, tie my shoe.

REFRAIN—faster (may be played over and over, without singing, for rhythmic play)

Jaw - bone walk and a jaw - bone talk, Jaw - bone eat with a knife and fork,

Left my jaw - bone in the cor - ner of the fence, And I have not seen my jaw-bone since.

138

Old Aunt Kate

Moderately fast ♩=112

Old Aunt Kate she bake a cake, She bake it 'hind the gar - den gate,

She sift the meal, she gim-me the dust, She bake the bread, she gim-me the crust,

She eat the meat, she gim-me the skin, And that's the way she took me in.

What Did You Have for Your Supper?

JIMMY RANDALL, MY SON

Moderate ♩. = 60

NORTH CAROLINA

It's what did you have for your sup-per,____ Jim-my Ran-dall, my son?

Oh, what did you have for your sup-per,____ my____ own lit-tle one?

Sweet milk and sweet par-snips, Mo-ther, make my bed soon,

For I'm tired at the heart and I want to lie down.

Baby Dear

SOUTH CAROLINA

Moderate ♩ = 80

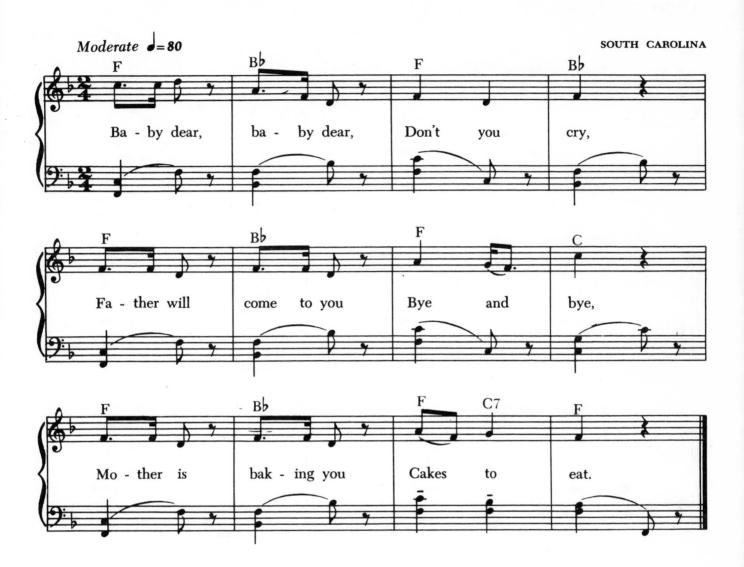

Ba - by dear, ba - by dear, Don't you cry,

Fa - ther will come to you Bye and bye,

Mo - ther is bak - ing you Cakes to eat.

Inclusion of friends and relations can make this a song without end.

Johnny Get Your Hair Cut

HEY BETTY MARTIN

PENNSYLVANIA

Fast ♩ = 108

Johnny get your hair cut, hair cut, hair cut,

Johnny get your hair cut, just like me.

Johnny get your hair cut, hair cut, hair cut,

Johnny get your hair cut, just like me. *Fine*

INTERLUDE I (may be played or whistled)

Return to the beginning or
continue to Interlude II

INTERLUDE II

D.C. al fine

2. Johnny get your gun and your sword and your pistol,
   Johnny get your gun and come with me.

3. Hey Betty Martin, tiptoe, tiptoe,
   Hey Betty Martin, tiptoe fine.

I Got a Letter This Morning

SOUTH CAROLINA

Moderately fast ♩ = 88

G   C   E min.

I got a let-ter this morn - ing, oh, yes,

G   C E min.   C

I got a let -ter this morn - ing, oh,_____ yes.

IMPROVISATION: Many new stanzas grow out of singing this song with children. Some may be used as finger plays. Others suggest simple dramatic play.

1. I wrote a letter this morning, oh, yes,
    I wrote a letter this morning, oh, yes.

2. I mailed a letter this morning, etc.

3. Who brought a letter this morning? etc.

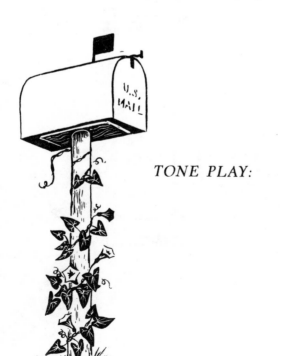

TONE PLAY:

Adult: I got a letter this morning . . .
Child: . . . . oh, yes.

Rose, Rose, and Up She Rises

Moderately fast ♩ = 100

KENTUCKY

Rose, Rose, and up she ris - es, Rose, Rose, and up she ris - es,

Rose, Rose, and up she ris - es So ear - ly in the morn - ing.

I wonder where Maria's gone,
I wonder where Maria's gone,
I wonder where Maria's gone,
So early in the morning.

IMPROVISATION: A waking-up song may grow out of stanza 1:

What shall we do with the sleepy Jackie? (3 times)
So early in the morning?

Wake him up and shake him up, (3 times)
So early in the morning.

Hoo-ray and up he rises, (3 times)
So early in the morning.
and so on.

An absence song may stem from stanza 2:

I wonder where Joanne has gone,
I wonder where has Arnold gone,
I wonder where Susanna's gone,
So early in the morning?

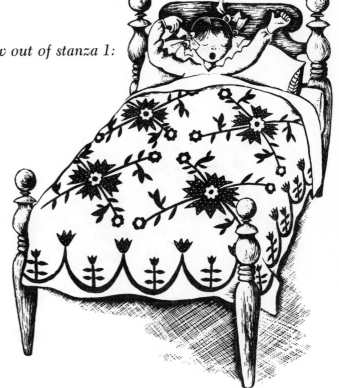

145

What'll We Do With the Baby?

KENTUCKY

Moderately fast ♩=84

What'll we do with the ba-by? What'll we do with the ba-by?

What'll we do with the ba-by? Oh, we'll wrap it up in cal-i-co,

Wrap it up in cal-i-co And send it to its pap-py-o.

146

Hush, Little Baby

ALABAMA

Fast ♩=120

Hush, lit-tle ba-by, don't say a word, Ma-ma's going to buy you a mock-ing bird.

2. If that mocking bird won't sing,
   Mama's going to buy you a diamond ring.

3. If that diamond ring turns brass,
   Mama's going to buy you a looking glass.

4. If that looking glass gets broke,
   Mama's going to buy you a billy goat.

5. If that billy goat won't pull,
   Mama's going to buy you a cart and bull.

6. If that cart and bull turn over,
   Mama's going to buy you a dog named Rover.

7. If that dog named Rover won't bark,
   Mama's going to buy you a horse and cart.

8. If that horse and cart fall down,
   You'll still be the prettiest girl in town.

TONE PLAY:

Adult: Mama's going to buy you a . . .
Child: . . . . mocking bird.

Pick a Bale of Cotton

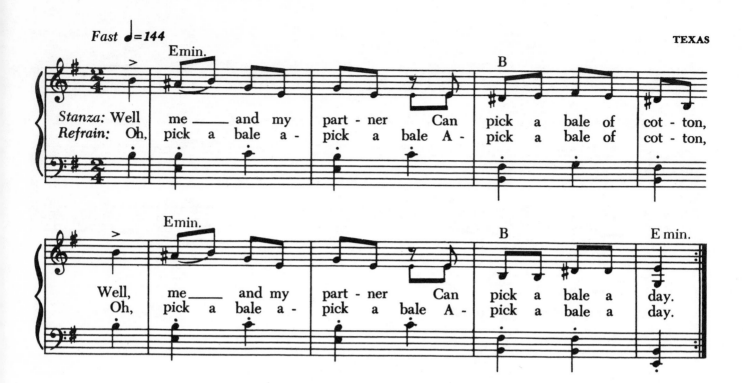

2. I can jump-a down and turn around
   And pick a bale of cotton,
   I can jump-a down and turn around
   And pick a bale a day.
   REFRAIN:

3. I had a little girl
   Could pick a bale of cotton,
   I had a little girl
   Could pick a bale a day.
   Refrain:

4. I'm on my way to Texas
   To pick a bale of cotton
   I'm on my way to Texas
   To pick a bale a day.
   Refrain:

   REFRAIN:

   Oh, pick a bale a-pick a bale
   A-pick a bale of cotton,
   Oh, pick a bale a-pick a bale
   A-pick a bale a day.

IMPROVISATION: Someone started singing one morning:

Well, me and my partner
Can put away our shovels,
Well, me and my partner
Can put them all away.

Oh, pick 'em up and pick 'em up
And pick 'em up together,
Oh, pick 'em up and pick 'em up
And put them all away.

This Old Hammer

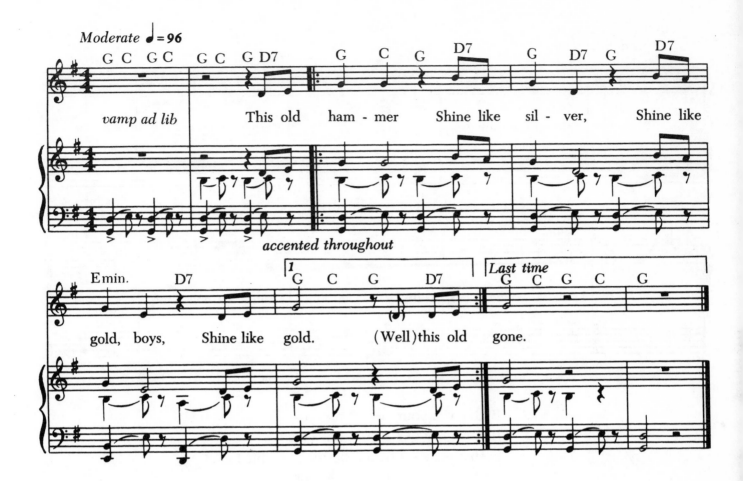

Moderate ♩=96

vamp ad lib

This old ham-mer Shine like sil-ver, Shine like gold, boys, Shine like gold. (Well)this old gone.

accented throughout

2. Well don't you hear that
   Hammer ringing?
   Drivin' in steel, boys,
   Drivin' in steel.

3. Can't find a hammer
   On this old mountain.
   Rings like mine, boys,
   Rings like mine.

4. I've been working
   On this old mountain
   Seven long years, boys,
   Seven long years.

5. I'm going back to
   Swannanoa Town-o,
   That's my home, boys,
   That's my home.

6. Take this hammer,
   Give it to the captain,
   Tell him I'm gone, boys,
   Tell him I'm gone.

RHYTHMIC and DRAMATIC PLAY: This Old Hammer and the John Henry songs are favorites for hammering. They may also form part of a railroad song-and-story sequence (see page 21).

The Train Is A-Coming

Moderate ♩=60

The train is a-com-ing, oh, yes, Train is a-com-ing, oh, yes,

Train is a-com-ing, train is a-com-ing, Train is a-com-ing, oh, yes.

2. Better get your ticket, oh, yes,
   Better get your ticket, oh, yes,
   Better get your ticket, better get your ticket,
   Better get your ticket, oh, yes.

3. Room for a-many more, oh, yes.

4. Jesus is conductor, oh, yes.

5. Train is a-leaving, oh, yes.

6. I'm on my way to heaven, oh, yes.

150

IMPROVISATION and RHYTHMIC PLAY: *Children like to play train. Sometimes they are cars—*

1. Steve is the engine, oh, yes, etc.
2. Joan is the coal car, oh, yes, etc.
   (*and so on, through all the
   kinds of cars that make up
   freight or passenger trains*)

—and sometimes they are trainmen—

3. Jock is the engineer, oh, yes, etc.
4. Pete is the brakeman, oh, yes, etc.
5. Barry is conductor, oh, yes, etc.
6. Patsy is a passenger, oh, yes, etc.

The train whistles before it starts:

(*Piano or children or both, on any one, two or three tones*)

And the engine eases the train out of the station, slow at first, then faster—and on around the countryside—perhaps to the music of The Little Black Train (*page 152*). Usually the train comes back safe and whole to the station. Sometimes it cannot resist running away to a wreck.

151

The Little Black Train

Very fast ♩ = 104–144

KENTUCKY

vamp ad lib

staccato throughout

There's a lit-tle black train___ a-com-ing,

Get all your busi-ness right,___

There's a lit-tle black train___ a-com-ing,

And it may be here to-night.

Ending

2. Oh, the little black train is a-coming,
   It's coming 'round the bend,
   You can hear those wheels a-moving
   And rattling through the land.

3. Oh, the little black train is a-coming,
   It's coming 'round the curve,
   A-whistling and a-blowing
   And straining every nerve.

When the Train Comes Along

SOUTH CAROLINA

When the train comes a - long, When the train comes a - long,

I'm going to meet you at the sta-tion When the train comes a - long.

2. If my mother ask for me,
   Tell her death done summon me,
   I'm going to meet her at the station
   When the train comes along.

3. If my father ask for me, etc.

4. If my brother ask for me, etc.
   and so on.

   When Jock's father left by plane for Mexico we sang about meeting him at the airport "when the plane comes along."

   If my father ask for me
   Tell him, look around for me,
   I'm going to meet him at the airport
   When the plane comes along.

153

John Henry

Moderately fast ♩=72

vamp ad lib When John Hen-ry was a-bout three days old,

Just a - sittin' on his pap - py's knee,

He gave one loud and lone-some cry:

"The___ ham-mer'll be the death of me,

The___ ham-mer'll be the death of me."

✱ *Beginning with stanza 3, omit this tone and substitute a quarter rest.*

When John Henry was about three days old,
A-sittin' on his pappy's knee,
He gave one loud and lonesome cry:
"The hammer'll be the death of me,
The hammer'll be the death of me."

Well, the captain said to John Henry one day:
"Gonna bring that steam drill 'round,
Gonna take that steam drill out on the job,
Gonna whop that steel on down,
Gonna whop that steel on down."

John Henry said to the captain:
"Well, the next time you go to town
Just bring me back a twelve-pound hammer
And I'll beat your steam drill down, etc."

John Henry said to the captain:
"Well, a man ain't nothin' but a man,
And before I let a steam drill beat me down
Gonna die with the hammer in my hand."

John Henry went to the tunnel,
And they put him in the lead to drive,
The rock so tall and John Henry so small,
He laid down his hammer and he cried.

John Henry said to his shaker:
"Shaker, why don't you sing?
For I'm swingin' twelve pounds from the hips
    on down,
Just listen to that cold steel ring."

John Henry told his captain:
"Look-a yonder what I see—
Your drill's done broke and your hole's done
    choke',
And you can't drive steel like me."

Well, the man that invented the steam drill,
He thought he was mighty fine,
But John Henry drove his fifteen feet,
And the steam drill only made nine.

John Henry looked up at the mountain,
And his hammer was striking fire,
Well, he hammered so hard that he broke his
    poor old heart,
He laid down his hammer and he died.

They took John Henry to the graveyard,
And they laid him in the sand,
Three men from the east and a woman from
    the west
Came to see that old steel-drivin' man.

They took John Henry to the graveyard,
And they laid him in the sand,
And every locomotive comes a-roarin' by
Says: "There lies a steel-drivin' man."

Every Monday Morning

MORE ABOUT JOHN HENRY

Moderately fast ♩=72

Well, ev' - ry ___ Mon - day ___ morn - ing,

When the blue-birds be - gin to sing, ___

You can hear those ham - mers a mile or ___ more,

You can hear John Hen- ry's ham-mer ring, oh Lawd - y,

Hear John Hen- ry's ham- mer ring.

This tune and first stanza are different from that of most John Henry songs. The stanzas below have been culled from several traditional sources.

2.   When John Henry was a little boy,
     He was on his way to school,
     Well, he looked at the teacher and this is what he said:
     "I want to learn how to hammer too, oh Lawdy,
     Want to learn how to hammer too."

3.   John Henry had a little woman,
     And her name was Polly Ann,
     When John Henry was sick and a-lying in his bed,
     Polly drove steel like a man, oh Lawdy,
     Polly drove steel like a man.

4.   John Henry had a little woman,
     Named Mary Magdalene,
     She would go to the tunnel and sing for John,
     Just to hear John Henry's hammer ring, oh Lawdy,
     Hear John Henry's hammer ring.

5.   John Henry had a little woman,
     And the dress she wore was blue,
     Well, the very last words I heard her say:
     "John Henry, I've been true to you, oh Lawdy,
     John Henry I've been true to you."

6.   John Henry told his little woman,
     "Will you fix my supper soon?
     Got ninety miles of track I've got to line,
     Got to line it by the light of the moon, oh Lawdy,
     Line it by the light of the moon."

7.   John Henry had a little baby,
     Held him in the palm of his hand,
     Well, the last words I heard that poor boy say:
     "My dad is a steel-driving man, oh Lawdy,
     Daddy is a steel-driving man."

8.   Some say John Henry come from England,
     And some say he's from Spain,
     But I say he's nothing but a Louisiana man,
     Just the leader of a steel-driving gang, oh Lawdy,
     Leader of a steel-driving gang.

Going Down to Town

LYNCHBURG TOWN

Moderately fast ♩=120

KENTUCKY

Refrain: I'm going down to town, I'm going down to town, I'm
Stanza: Times a-get-ting hard, Mon-ey get-ting scarce,

going down to the Lynch-burg town To take my to-bac-co down.
Pay me for them to-bac-co, boys, And I will leave this place. D.C.

2. Master had an old gray horse,
   Took him down to town,
   Sold him for a half a dollar
   And only a quarter down.
   Refrain:

3. Old Eli was a rich old man,
   He was richer than a king,
   He made me beat the old tin pan
   While Sary Jane would sing.
   Refrain:

4. Old Eli brought a little girl,
   He fetched her from the South,
   Her hair was wrapped so very tight
   That she couldn't shut her mouth.
   Refrain:

REFRAIN:

I'm going down to town,
I'm going down to town,
I'm going down to the Lynchburg town
To take my tobacco down.

5. Once I had an old black hen,
   She laid behind the door,
   Every day she laid three eggs,
   And Sunday she laid more.
   Refrain:

6. Oh, I went down to town,
   And went into the store,
   And every pretty girl in town
   Came running to the door.
   Refrain:

DRAMATIC PLAY: Children often draw on the tobacco story for dramatic play. Sometimes they use the refrain as a shopping song—going down to town, play-shopping from store to store, then returning to tell or sing about each thing they have bought.

1. I'm going down to town,
   I'm going down to town,
   I'm going down to Silver Spring
   To get my shopping done.

   The music may be played ad lib until someone is ready to sing about coming home again.

2. I'm coming home from town, etc.
   I've got my shopping done.

Sailing in the Boat

Moderately fast ♩=80

Sail - ing in the boat when the tide runs high,

Sail - ing in the boat when the tide runs high,

Sail - ing in the boat when the tide runs high,

Wait - ing for the pret - ty girls to come by'm bye.

Here she comes so fresh and fair,
Sky-blue eyes and curly hair,
Rosy in cheek, dimple in her chin,
Say, young man, but you can't come in.

*RHYTHMIC PLAY: Children find different ways of sailing in the
boat. One boy was careful to moor himself to the dock when he got
back. Several others thought of returning with cargoes. Others arched
their arms to make drawbridges.*

Blow, Boys, Blow

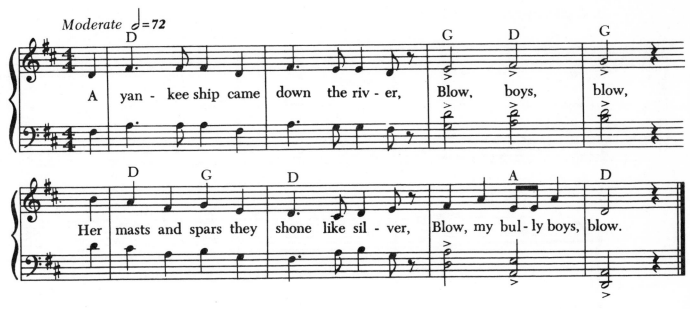

Moderate ♩=72

A yan - kee ship came down the riv - er, Blow, boys, blow,

Her masts and spars they shone like sil - ver, Blow, my bul - ly boys, blow.

2. Who do you think is the captain of her?
   Blow, boys, blow;
   Why, Bully Hayes is the captain of her,
   Blow, my bully boys, blow.

3. And what do you think they've got for dinner? etc.
   Pickled eel's feet and bullock's liver, etc.

4. And how do you know she's a Yankee liner? etc.
   The Stars and Stripes float out behind her, etc.

Fire Down Below

2. There's fire up aloft,
    There's fire down below,
    Fire in the galley,
    The cook didn't know.
    Chorus:

3. There's fire in the forepeak,
    Fire down below,
    Fire in the chain-plates,
    The bo'sun didn't know.
    Chorus:

Penelope likes, too, to sing of fire in other places besides ships—in the fireplace, the kitchen stove, the toaster, a cigarette.

Sally Go Round the Sunshine

SOUTH CAROLINA

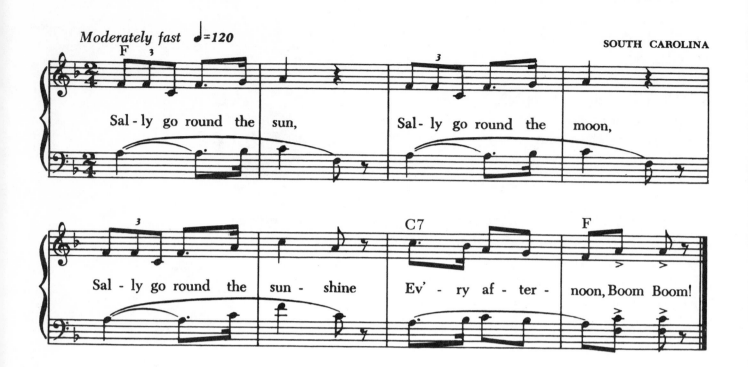

Moderately fast ♩=120

F

Sal - ly go round the sun, Sal - ly go round the moon,

Sal - ly go round the sun - shine Ev' - ry af - ter - noon, Boom Boom!

C7   F

Children join hands, form a circle. The circle may move to the left (the sun), to the right (the moon), to the left again (the sunshine) and fall down at "Boom Boom."

164

This Old Man

NEW YORK

Moderately fast ♩=100

This old man, he played one, He played knick knack on his thumb, Knick knack pad-dy whack, give your dog a bone, This old man came roll-ing home.

2. This old man, he played two,
   He played knick knack on his shoe,
   Knick knack, paddy whack, give your dog a bone,
   This old man came rolling home.

3. This old man, he played three,
   He played knick knack on his knee.

4. This old man, he played four,
   He played knick knack on the floor.

5. This old man, he played five,
   He played knick knack on his hives.

6. This old man, he played six,
   He played knick knack on his sticks.

7. This old man, he played seven,
   He played knick knack up to heaven.

8. This old man, he played eight,
   He played knick knack on his pate.

9. This old man, he played nine,
   He played knick knack on his spine.

10. This old man, he played ten,
    He played knick knack now and then.

Skip-a to My Lou

SHOO-LI-LOO

WAGONS

2. Pull her up and down in the little red wagon,
   Pull her up and down in the little red wagon,
   Pull her up and down in the little red wagon,
   Skip-a to my lou, my darling.
   Refrain:

3. Teeter up and down in the little red wagon, etc.

ANIMALS

4. Pig in the parlor, what'll I do? etc.
5. Cat in the buttermilk, lapping up cream, etc.
6. Rats in the bread tray, how they chew, etc.
7. Chickens in the garden, shoo shoo shoo, etc.
8. Rabbit in the cornfield, big as a mule, etc.
9. Cow in the kitchen, moo cow moo, etc.
10. Hogs in the potato patch, rooting up corn, etc.

REFRAIN:

Lou, lou, skip-a to my lou,
Lou, lou, skip-a to my lou,
Lou, lou, skip-a to my lou,
Skip-a to my lou, my darling.

GOING TO MARKET

11. Going to market two by two, etc.
12. Dad's old hat and Mama's old shoe, etc.
13. Back from market, what did you do? etc.
14. Had a glass of buttermilk, one and two, etc.

SKIPPING AND CATCHING

15. Skip skip, skip-a to my lou, etc.
16. Skip a little faster, that won't do, etc.
17. Going to Texas, come along too, etc.
18. Lost my partner, what'll I do? etc.
19. I'll get another one prettier than you, etc.
20. Catch that red bird, skip-a to my lou, etc.
21. If you can't get a red bird, take a blue, etc.
22. If you can't get a blue bird, black bird'll do, etc.

IMPROVISATION: This song has hundreds of stanzas and is always picking up new ones. One collector alone gives 150, from which the above 22 were selected as encouragement to further improvisation. The phrase "skip-a to my lou" has numerous variants, such as skip to ma lou, skip to my lula, skip come a lou, shoo li loo, shoo la lay.

GAME: "Skip-a to My Lou" can be played in many ways. The following is one of the simplest: The children form a circle with a child in the center. They clap and sing while he skips around. At the refrain "Lou lou," he chooses a child from the circle to skip with him. At the end of the refrain the first child returns to the circle and the second child repeats the game pattern while a new stanza is sung.

Still simpler game patterns can be used.

When I Was a Young Maid

HA HA, THIS-A-WAY

KENTUCKY

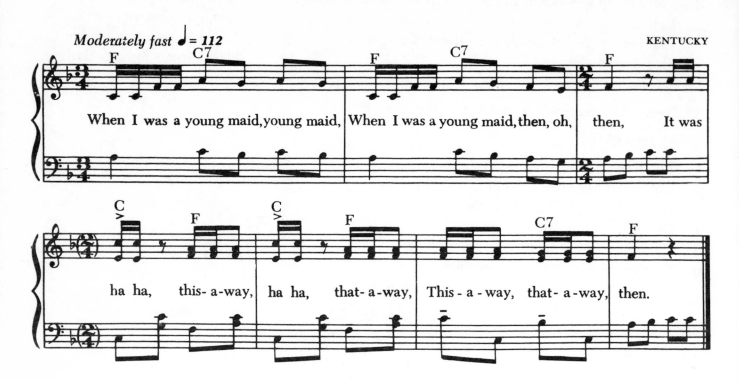

Moderately fast ♩ = 112

When I was a young maid, young maid, When I was a young maid, then, oh, then, It was

ha ha, this-a-way, ha ha, that-a-way, This-a-way, that-a-way, then.

Children's choice of occupation shows wide range—they are carpenters, shoemakers, bricklayers, hairdressers, taxi drivers, firemen, animals, insects. Sometimes they form a circle, with center player changing from stanza to stanza and initiating in pantomime his choice of activity for the circle to imitate. The song is, however, especially liked when acted out simply, in free unpatterned play.

The Closet Key

I've lost the clos-et key In that la-dy's gar-den,

I've lost the clos-et key In that la-dy's gar-den.

2. Help me to find the closet key,
   In that lady's garden,
   Help me to find the closet key,
   In that lady's garden.

3. I've found the closet key
   In that lady's garden,
   I've found the closet key
   In that lady's garden.

Very small children use this easily chanted song for informal hiding-and-finding play. Older children may like to play it as indicated in the folklore collection in which it was found:

The children form a ring, as in "dropping the handkerchief," but with hands behind them. One child with a key walks around the ring and places the key in someone's hands. The walker leads the singing of stanzas 1 and 2 (with all children joining in). The child to whom the key was given then leads the singing of stanza 3 (with all children joining in). He then proceeds to walk around the ring himself, singing stanza 1, and the whole process is repeated.

Built My Lady a Fine Brick House

Moderately fast ♩=108   TEXAS

Built my la-dy a fine brick house, Built it in a gar-den, I

put her in but she jumped out, So fare ye well, my darl-ing.

REFRAIN (may be omitted)

Oh, swing a la-dy ump - tum, swing a la-dy round,

Swing a la-dy ump - tum and prom-e -nade a -round.

RHYTHMIC PLAY: In one room there was a low bench under a long row of windows. Children stood on it to look outdoors. They liked to sing this song while they jumped off (or were jumped) one by one. If there were many children, we sang the jumping phrase over and over without finishing the song—until the last child was off the bench—

> I put him in but he jumped out,
> I put her in but she jumped out,
> *and so on.*

Someone always climbed up again to try for a second turn.

GAMES: Any number of simple game patterns may be improvised. One group of children joined hands in a ring and all jumped in toward the center, then back out again. Another group formed a ring around a center child, who listened for the words "but she jumped out" and jumped out of the ring. At another time the center child jumped "out" in front of some child in the ring, who then took her place in the center for a repetition of the game.

171

Where Oh Where Is Pretty Little Susie?

PAWPAW PATCH

2. Come on, boys, let's go find her,
   Come on, boys, let's go find her,
   Come on, boys, let's go find her,
   'Way down yonder in the pawpaw patch.

GAME: Even two-year-olds like to make a hiding game of stanzas 1 and 2. One child hides during stanza 1 while the others cover their eyes. At "Come on, boys," the group runs to find him. Sometimes an improvised third stanza brings everyone back again.

3. Come on, boys, bring her back again (3 times),
   Way down yonder in the pawpaw patch.

Jingle at the Windows
TIDEO

Moderately fast ♩ = 120

C

Skip one win-dow, Ti - de - o, Skip two windows, Ti - de - o,

F   C

Skip three win - dows, Ti - de - o, Jing-le at the win - dows, Ti - de - o.

C   F C   F   C

Jing-ling jing - ling jing-ling Jo, Jing-le at the win-dows, Ti - de - o.

At Christmas time this old play-party song becomes a companion to the favorite Jingle Bells. Various game patterns may be improvised if desired, but free rhythmic play—with or without bells on ankles or wrists—is perhaps most loved.

173

Adam Had Seven Sons

Moderately fast ♩=120

Ad - am had sev - en sons, Sev - en sons had Ad - am,

And they all were bright and gay, And they did what Ad - am say,

"Let's all do this, Let's all do this," says Ad - am.

In Mississippi the game is played as a circle game, with Adam in the center. At "Let's all do this," Adam makes any sort of motion he wishes, and the circle imitates him.

Here Sits a Monkey

Moderate ♩ = 120

MISSISSIPPI

Oh, here sits a mon-key in the chair, chair, chair, She

lost all the true loves she had last year, So

rise up-on your feet and greet the first you meet, the

pret-ti-est girl I know

GAME: *The children form a circle around a center child, who sits in a chair or on the floor. They march or skip around her, singing. At the proper time she rises and chooses someone from the circle to take her place in the chair, and the game is repeated. Each new center child may be a different animal or thing—giraffe, zebra, snake, worm. One child wanted to be a piano. It is easier to remember to rise and choose if the circle stops marching at "So rise upon your feet" and starts clapping while continuing to sing.*

Go to Sleepy

Moderate ♩.= 88

SOUTH CAROLINA

1. Go to sleep - y, ba - by, bye, ____
2. Bye - o ba - by, bye, ____

Go to sleep - y, ba - by, bye, ____
Bye - o ba - by, bye, ____

Ma - ma's gone to the mail - boat, Ma - ma's gone to the mail - boat,
Fa - ther's gone to the mail boat, Fa - ther's gone to the mail - boat,

Ending

Bye. ____
Bye. ____

Monday Morning Go to School

THE TWO BROTHERS

Moderate ♩=76   NORTH CAROLINA

Mon-day morn-ing go to school. Fri-day eve-ning home,

Bro-ther, comb my sweet-heart's hair As we go march-ing home.

Brother, will you play me a game of ball?
Brother, will you toss a stone?
Brother, will you play another game
As we go marching home?

Hush 'n' Bye

ALL THE PRETTY LITTLE PONIES

Moderate ♩ = 60

SOUTH CAROLINA

Hush 'n' bye, don't you cry Oh, you pret-ty lit-tle ba - by,

When you wake you'll have sweet cake, And all the pret-ty lit-tle pon - ies, A

brown and a gray and a black and a bay, And all the pret-ty lit-tle pon-ies.

When we sang a song from Alabama about "all the pretty little ponies," Virginia Vose's mother remembered a similar song which her nurse had sung to her when she was a child in South Carolina. She sang us her version, and we all liked it so much that we learned it. It became a favorite.

Turtle Dove

NORTH CAROLINA

Moderate ♩ = 60

Poor lit - tle tur - tle dove, sit - ting in a pine,

Mourn-ing for its own true love, and why not me for mine, for mine, And why not me for mine?

(Copyright 1929 by Carl Fischer, Inc., New York.)

2. Hogs in the pen, and corn to feed them on,
   All I want is a pretty little girl to feed them when I'm gone, oh gone,
   To feed them when I'm gone.

3. I went up on the mountain to give my horn a blow,
   And every girl in the valley said, "Yonder comes my beau, oh beau,
   Oh, yonder comes my beau."

4. I'm not going to marry in the fall, I'm going to marry in the spring,
   I'm going to marry a pretty little girl that wears a silver ring, oh
       ring,
   That wears a silver ring.

Mary Had a Baby

Moderately slow ♩=60

SOUTH CAROLINA

Ma-ry had a ba-by, Aye, Lord,

Ma-ry had a ba-by, Aye, my Lord, Ma-ry had a ba-by, Aye, Lord, The

peo-ple keep a-com-ing and the train done gone.

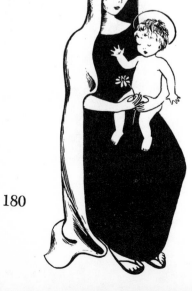

2. What did she name him? Aye, Lord.
   What did she name him? Aye, my Lord.
   What did she name him? Aye, Lord.
   The people keep a-coming and the train done gone.
3. Named him Jesus, etc.
4. Where was he born?, etc.
5. Born in a stable, etc.
6. Where did they lay him?, etc.
7. Laid him in a manger, etc.

A group of older children carried the song on and on through all the details they knew, from the shepherds and the star to the flight into Egypt.

Jesus Borned in Bethlea

VIRGINIA

Children have improvised with ease many new stanzas out of their knowledge of the Christmas story. Only two unrhymed lines are needed.

The Cherry Tree Carol

KENTUCKY
(composite of two versions)

As Ma-ry and Jo-seph were a-walk-ing the green,

There were ap-ples and cher-ries a-plen-ty to be seen,

There were ap-ples and cher-ries a-plen-ty to be seen. 2. Then me.

2. Then Mary spoke to Joseph,
   So meek and so mild,
   "Joseph, gather me some cherries
   For me and my child.
   Joseph, gather me some cherries
   For me and my child."

3. Lord Jesus spoke a few words
   All down unto them:
   "Bow down, you lofty cherry tree,
   Let my mammy gather some."

4. The cherry tree bowed low down,
   Low down to the ground,
   And Mary gathered cherries
   While Joseph stood around.

5. Then Joseph took Mary
   All on his right knee:
   "Pray tell me, little baby,
   When your birthday will be?"

6. "On old Christmas morning
   My birthday shall be
   When the hills and high mountains
   Shall bow unto me."

Classified Indices

RHYTHMIC INDEX

GENERAL
The following songs adapt themselves with special ease to a variety of activities and rhythmic
change, such as walking, running,
hopping, jumping, skipping, et
cetera. Ten sample rhythmic variations have been given with the
song *Jim Along Josie.*

CLAPPING AND RHYTHM BAND
Clapping makes a natural accompaniment for most of these songs.
The following are especially well
suited to clapping and to use with
rhythm band.

GALLOPING

HAMMERING, KNOCKING, TAPPING

JUMPING, HOPPING

MARCHING (see WALKING)

RIDING

Other Indices

Many songs can be used as tone plays and finger plays. The following are good examples.

Index of Song Titles and First Lines

Page numbers of the songs are indicated in **bold figures.**